Behind the paperbacks on Griffin's shelf, Phoenix noticed several hardback books almost hidden. Numb, she read the titles: Approaching Death: Twenty-six Case Histories. The next book was titled: Attitudes Toward Terminal Illnesses; the last was When the End is Near.

Stunned, puzzled, then violently angry, she whirled around and headed for the bathroom door.

Griffin was in the tub, soaping away happily, when Phoenix kicked the bathroom door.

"Goddam you," she screamed, "How the hell did you find out? Who gave you the right to snoop around in my life?"

Griffin was utterly confused. "What are you talking about?"

"Why did you do it? I loved you, you sneaky bastard, and you're playing some sick game!"

The heavy books clobbered Griffin one by one as she hurled them at him. He picked one up, read the title and turned white. Before he could protest, the front door slammed. Phoenix was gone, and she wasn't coming back.

Griffin
Loves
Phoenix

A novel by
John Hill

WARNER BOOKS

A Warner Communications Company

WARNER BOOKS EDITION
First Printing: March, 1976

Copyright © 1976 by John Hill
All rights reserved

Warner Books, Inc., 75 Rockefeller Plaza,
New York, N.Y. 10019

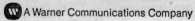 A Warner Communications Company

Printed in the United States of America

Not associated with Warner Press, Inc. of Anderson, Indiana

To Pat Clipner.
Desideratum et libelli virorum.

Acknowledgments

The story behind this story is full of nice people. My sincere thanks to Norman Kurland and Leonard Hanzer, for gambling on the kid; to Tony Thomas and Paul Junger Witt, for keeping the faith; and to Peter Falk, Jill Clayburgh, and Daryl Duke for their brilliant contributions to the film which I've used in the novel, where, of course, I'll get full credit.—J.H.

Prologue

FEBRUARY, 1975—
CALIFORNIA DESERT

The driver squinted into the desert sunlight as he stopped his car beside the empty highway. He couldn't reach his new sunglasses from where he was sitting. His new sunglasses were in the men's room of a Texaco station, eighty miles back.

He got out, slammed the door, marched back to the big camper-trailer hitched to his car, and jerked the door open.

"Now what?"

A transistor radio was blaring from inside, a large dog started barking, trying to get out, and two boys, ages eight and twelve, started yelling.

"Bobby slugged me," hollered the eight-year-old. "Can we get out?"

"No, I didn't, honest, Dad," yelled the twelve-year-old who had just slugged his brother. "Can we?"

The man was too busy shoving the large dog back inside to answer. His wife, Jean, appeared in the doorway.

"No, stay inside!" she snapped. The kids protested. The dog barked. The radio blared. The man tried to count to ten. He made it to three.

"Somebody hold the ~~damn~~ dog!" he yelled. The boys dragged it back inside.

"That rattle still bothers me," Jean said. Only she had been able to hear the rattle.

"Okay. I'll stop again at the next service station," the man sighed. They just looked at each other.

He was thirty-seven, average build, handsome in a rugged sort of way, and usually in a lot better mood.

She was thirty-five, mildly attractive, but seriously considering plumpness. She was a pleasant enough person; if you married her, you would look back upon that decision as a good one, but not a great one.

"You never said it would get this hot," she said.

"Deserts are hot," he said. "I can't help it. That's how they make them. That's so you can tell them from other places."

"Don't get sarcastic. This trip to Yosemite was your idea, remember? So we could all be together again? Well, we're sure together. How do you like it?" Then she slowly closed the camper door. In his face.

An hour later, while trying to find some music he liked on the car radio, the man glanced in his rear-view mirror. In the front camper window, Jean held up a small, crudely lettered sign: THE CHEMICAL TOILET OVERFLOWED ON THE CAR-BINGO GAME.

He snapped off the radio. Again, he pulled over to the side of the road.

Thirty-two miles later, still getting bad country music and local commercials, another sign appeared in his rear-view mirror: CAN YOU STOP AND WALK THE DOG?

Strangely calm, he stopped the car on the shoulder of the highway and wrote on the back of a road map in big, bold strokes. He got out and walked to the back of his car, ignoring the beautiful, dark hills that make up the horizon of the American West. There were no towns or people in sight, only some "purple mountains' majesty."

He bent over the connection where the camper was hitched to his car.

Above him, Jean impatiently tapped on the camper window, holding up the sign that asked him to walk the dog. The man straightened up, looked at her, then slapped his own homemade sign against the glass, filling the window: I DON'T HAVE TIME.

The message stayed there a few moments, until the wind made it flutter away, revealing the man driving off in the car, leaving an unhitched camper on the side of the road.

Jean's mouth slowly opened as she stared out of the window.

Picking up speed, never looking back, the man turned on his radio. Fast, upbeat music was right there, waiting for him. He smiled as he passed a sign. "Los Angeles, 182 Miles."

The man's name was Jeffrey Alan Griffin. He was humming to himself as he drove away. He was thirty-seven years old, not going on thirty-eight.

Chapter One

MARCH, 1976—LOS ANGELES

Like all hospitals, it smelled like a test tube from an unsuccessful experiment, but George Griffin didn't notice.

He stood in a doorway marked "Administration." He was a handsome man of forty-three, and wore a dark suit and tie, and a distant, stunned expression.

"Yes? May I help you?"

The young woman's voice was as pleasantly sterile as her office. She was a pretty, efficient young woman with a constipated hairdo and a desk full of paperwork.

When George didn't answer right away, she recognized the disoriented, vaguely guilty look on his face.

"You wish to sign a Release of Remains?" she asked.

George nodded and slowly sat down. The administrator briskly got out several forms and a small paper sack, stapled shut.

"You're a blood relative of the deceased . . . Jeffrey Alan Griffin?"

"I'm his brother."

There was a flurry of official forms and carbon paper.

"Please sign where I've X-ed, here . . . and here . . . and here."

George did as he was told. She smoothly slid a new form under his pen and began a rapid monotone.

"One man's wristwatch, Bulova, gold inlay; seven keys; one keychain with laminated three-leaf clover; one wallet, brown, cash content, twenty-two dollars. Please sign this Release of Property."

George slowly signed. The paperwork magically slid away, the pen disappeared, and he was left holding the bag.

"There you are," said the woman, "and please accept County General's sincerest sympathy for your recent loss."

George slowly looked up at her, then back to the paper sack, then up at her again. In the uncomfortable silence, she smiled and waited. George got to his feet a few moments later and started for the door. She was back at her paperwork before he was out of her office.

"As his lawyer, and as his friend, I tried to tell him," the fast-talking man explained, with a lot of arm waving, from behind his big desk. "I mean, you just *can't* leave this kind of provision in a will . . ."

As the lawyer searched his papers for the exact wording, George Griffin sat and stared at the plush office. It was a forest of dark mahogany paneling.

"Here. Here it is," the lawyer said. "I mean, I've heard unusual last requests before, but this . . . 'to be cremated, my ashes placed in a heavy, tacky, brass urn, then taken up in a small plane and dropped over a greenhouse.'"

The lawyer finished reading, gesturing to show that what he had just read was ridiculous, and began to chuckle, waiting for George to join him.

George just sat there, numb.

The lawyer turned the chuckle into a cough. Leaning forward, looking serious, he elaborately put his hands together on top of the desk.

"Mr. Griffin, your brother's estate already has *eleven* automobile damage claims to settle, right? I mean, *actually* dropping it would cause the wife's suit, the florist's, the FAA raising hell—"

"I know it can't be done," said George, sadly. "I

14

just wish . . ." He paused, and was silent, overwhelmed by all the things he wished.

George stalled around all morning, before finally making himself drive to the beach. He had been to his brother's apartment twice before and had planned to fly in from Albuquerque to visit him again, but had put the trip off too long.

He remembered a quote that said if everyone knew they were all going to die in five minutes, the phone lines would be jammed with people telling each other how much they loved them.

The young surfer-type, who looked more like a tenant than the landlord, let him into the apartment, staring at the strange redwood box George carried.

"Sure sorry about everything," the landlord said, "but you said you would finish getting the place cleaned up by now . . ."

George looked around the room. It was a small, cheap apartment. His brother Jeff had considerately packed up half of his clothes and stuff in neatly labeled cardboard boxes. The other half was still junk and confusion. George was lost in memory for a few moments.

"I'll take care of everything today," he finally said.

"You know, a place right on the beach . . . this time of year . . ."

George turned and stared at the landlord, who then nodded and hurried away, closing the door.

George looked at the stacks of old clothes, the half-packed dishes, the books and magazines strewn on the floor. He set the redwood box he was carrying down gently. Then, smiling wryly, he spoke to it.

"Thirty years later, you're still leaving your room a mess and I'm getting in trouble for it."

On a nearby shelf, he saw an exquisite little glass-blown winged horse, a dead baby octopus floating in a little sealed jar, and an empty goldfish bowl.

Still snooping around, George opened a closet, pushed aside some of his brother's clothes, and noticed some dresses and women's clothes also there, right at home.

George smiled to himself; women had always liked Jeff.

"Got anything to drink?" he said to the redwood box. He walked into the kitchen and opened the refrigerator.

"One can, man's beer; Budweiser, red design, tall, cold," he said, in a monotone like a hospital administrator. He popped open the beer and wandered back into the living room.

He noticed a snapshot pinned to the kitchen wall. He took it down and studied it, as he slouched in a big overstuffed chair, sipping his beer.

The photograph showed Jeff Griffin hamming it up with someone, doing a deadpan imitation of Grant Wood's "American Gothic." Griffin held up a stolen "No Parking" sign instead of a pitchfork, looking completely serious, wearing an old-fashioned beanie with a twirler on top. Beside him, playing the salt-of-the-earth woman, her arm linked in his, was a very shapely young woman whose face was hidden by a catcher's mask.

George put the photograph aside, staring away, blinking a little. He picked up a kite and some string that were beside the chair. He smiled, and took a sip of his beer, looking at the kite.

"Jesus, Jeff . . . why you?"

He stared at the kite, as though waiting for an answer . . .

JANUARY, 1975—ALBUQUERQUE

Jeff Griffin felt real fear for the first time the moment Dr. Feinberg lit a cigarette. There was already one burning in his ashtray on the desk.

"We have the results of your second biopsy," Dr. Feinberg said, quickly putting out the second cigarette. He studied a folder for a moment, then sat on the couch beside Griffin.

"Isn't this where I say 'Give it to me straight, Doc'?" Griffin asked, with a nervous smile.

16

Dr. Feinberg smiled at this briefly, dropped his eyes, then forced himself to look right at Griffin.

"Mr. Griffin, the second specialist concurs, even after completely new tests. You have a particularly virulent form of cancer called melanoma."

The doctor paused. Griffin just looked at him, without change of expression. Dr. Feinberg continued.

"A shower of small cancers developed along your left chest wall and back. There are more than eighty lesions, malignant, and completely inoperable."

Dr. Feinberg paused again.

"I recommend immunotherapy, a relatively new form of treatment which seeks to stimulate immunity so the body can rid itself of the tumor and prevent further spread of the cancer. You are wondering if it will save you. It will not. It has spread too far for us to do anything but try to arrest the growth and give you more time. You will live about a year, but not much more."

At this point, the doctor faltered.

"When the pain begins . . . there are treatments that will help . . . a little." Dr. Feinberg stopped and leaned back, the rough part over.

Griffin simply looked at Dr. Feinberg and spoke softly.

"I'm thirty-seven years old."

The words sounded very loud in the quiet room. Dr. Feinberg looked back at Griffin. The two men didn't say anything.

When Griffin left the medical building, he walked half a block, then realized his car was parked the other way.

Reaching his car, he started to get in, then noticed something and stared at the front of his car.

He had a flat tire.

Griffin half-smiled to himself, shaking his head a little. He looked up, then back at the flat tire, still shaking his head.

The rest of his day, however, went pretty well.

In the United States alone, roughly 365,000 people die of cancer every year—a thousand people a day. In another city, someone else received similar news, but had a somewhat different reaction . . .

JANUARY, 1975–SEATTLE

Dr. Glenn, a short, balding, middle-aged man, had set a box of Kleenex on his desk just before her appointment.

"Well, I'm sorry but you're wrong," stated Sarah Phoenix, a very attractive woman in her early thirties.

Dr. Glenn sighed and tried again. "Miss Phoenix—"

"You're wrong," Phoenix concluded, dismissing the entire subject with a shrug and a nervous puff of her cigarette.

Dr. Glenn quietly sighed again, wishing he weren't so conscious of how sexy she was at a time like this. Miss Phoenix, in his opinion, had one of those very special female bodies where you couldn't quite explain why everything fitted together so well, but it did.

He looked once again at the lab reports, graphs, and X rays on his desk, trying to think of what to say next.

"I'm very sorry, but we're positive."

"It's out of the question," said Phoenix, with a fake laugh. "You've got your files confused. The lab screwed up . . . I don't know."

She paced around the room in front of his desk. The afternoon rain on the window of Dr. Glenn's office lent a melodramatic touch that was almost embarrassing.

"Miss Phoenix, I don't tell a patient something like this unless every possible—"

She interrupted, not listening, continuing to pace.

"Five years I love the guy. Five years, then he gets married a month ago. Some pseudo-intellectual bitch from the Village. I decide the farthest away from Manhattan I can get is Seattle. *Seattle,* for Christ's sake. Can't get a job. Rains every day. I come see you, you make me take all those *goddam tests . . .*" She paced faster. Her volume increased until she was yelling. Suddenly, she hurled her purse across the room, startling Dr. Glenn. Lipstick, gum, compact, pens, and other things spilled out. She marched over and quickly threw them back into her purse, continuing to yell. ". . . a bunch of goddam stupid tests, it's still raining, you keep me sitting in your tacky waiting room with the flocked wallpaper and the back-fucking issues of *National Geographic* and *Redbook,* then when you finally drag my ass in here, you try to tell me I'll be dead in a year!" She was standing now, purse in hand, screaming at him, tears in her eyes.

"You sanctimonious little jerk! You think you're the only doctor in the world?" She whirled around, charged out of his office, and slammed the door loudly.

Startled, Dr. Glenn jumped a little.

As he wryly decided she might not need the Kleenex after all, he heard his nurse make the mistake of speaking to her. All he heard from the reception room was Phoenix's answer.

"Make another appointment? You stupid old witch, don't stand there in your goddammed orthopedic pantyhose and tell me to make another appointment! Why don't you go somewhere and get that wart removed!"

The main door in the reception room slammed shut. All was quiet and still.

Then behind Dr. Glenn, completely without ceremony, one of his framed diplomas fell to the floor, the glass shattered.

Dr. Glenn jumped.

Chapter Two

JANUARY, 1975—ALBUQUERQUE

The first thing Griffin did after getting the news from Dr. Feinberg, and fixing his flat tire, was to head straight for his safety-deposit box and to make sure his papers and insurance forms were in order.

The second thing he did was to have a hot fudge sundae.

He'd planned to have just a cup of coffee, but was amused to find himself reaching for the little pink packs of sugar substitute. He'd been trying to lose another five pounds. What the hell, he thought to himself, the first of many times that phrase was to start going through his mind. So he ordered a hot fudge sundae, with extra whipped cream and extra nuts.

He sat there, really enjoying it, then suddenly couldn't remember what day it was. This suddenly became very important to him, and he asked the waitress. Finding out it was Tuesday instead of Monday had a strange effect on him. The significance of the hot fudge sundae hit him. His hand began to shake a little. He left, without finishing it.

He drove to a public park, one in south Albuquerque he had always liked, thought about going to a movie, and even considered going back to the office for the rest of the day. He finally realized what he was really doing: avoiding going back to his new, one-bedroom furnished apartment. There was something about facing an empty apartment for his remaining days and nights that made him panic.

He drove straight for his home.

It was a nice suburban neighborhood. His two boys were playing basketball in the driveway, using the hoop he'd put up a few years before, a foot too low. Beside the driveway, as though it had taken root, was a big new camper-trailer he and Jean had bought only a week before they separated. For four months it had sat there. Funny they hadn't sold it, he thought to himself, as he parked in front. He realized he and Jean used to talk so much about going camping as a family that it might have become a symbol. Good, he thought, I'm going to need every trick in the book.

His twelve-year-old son, Bobby, was playing about half as well as he could, letting his eight-year-old brother Billy have more of a chance. George used to give me the same break, Griffin remembered. He watched his sons play.

Bobby hadn't yet shown any interest in anything special, but he was bright and personable. Maybe he'd become a salesman. Little Billy already had a real interest in science. He loved his chemistry set and the illustrated children's biology books Griffin had bought him. Billy might just be a scientist someday.

"Hi, guys!" Griffin suddenly yelled, clapping his hands together, walking onto the driveway. "If someone will just pass the old guy the ball, we'll play—"

"C'mon, Dad," said Bobby, who continued dribbling. "We just started a game. We're playing one-on-one."

"Yeah, Dad," Billy chimed in, "we're playing one-on-one."

Billy stole the ball away from his big brother and double-dribbled past Griffin, who had to step out of their way as the game continued, frantically.

Griffin heard the front door open. Jean came outside, carefully closed the door behind her, walked over to Griffin, and ushered him around to the side of the house.

Griffin smiled at her; she wasn't smiling back.

"You're supposed to call first."

"Yeah, well, I was in the area so . . . uh, is there . . . I mean, have you got, uh . . ."

"Company? Yes, I do." Her tone remained neutral.

There was an awkward pause. The boys continued playing basketball, twenty feet away, out of earshot.

"Are the boys all right?"

"You just saw them Saturday."

This wasn't going the way Griffin wanted it to. If he had only about 365 days left, that was 365 dinners he'd be eating alone.

"Jeff, if there's nothing wrong or anything, can't you please come back some other—"

"No, there's nothing wrong. I just . . . yes, there is. This is wrong. I want us all back together."

"Jeff," she said, tiredly.

Griffin had a sudden burst of excitement.

"Look, remember that camping trip you wanted us all to take just before . . . you know, uh . . ."

"Separation is not a dirty word, Jeff. Lots of people—"

"Okay, okay, anyway, remember how the boys were looking forward to it? Well, now I'd love to go, too! Let's do it, Jean! Finally getting the camper out on the road will really give us a chance to be together and talk."

"It's different now, Jeff," Jean said, unconsciously glancing back at the house. "Can't we talk about this some other time?"

"It'll be good for all of us. Change of scenery, fresh air—"

"You hate fresh air."

"I want us together. Now." His tone of voice sounded different.

"What's happened to you? You're acting . . . so . . ." Griffin hurried on.

"Just say you'll think about it. The kids would have a ball . . . and we might love it, too." Griffin suddenly stopped trying to convince her. He'd been too good a salesman not to know when to shut up. She watched the boys for a moment, thinking.

Griffin looked at her and remembered how they got

23

the giggles during the wedding ceremony and how much in love they were during their first years of marriage. And suddenly, it wasn't just that he didn't want to eat alone or be alone or even die alone. He wanted to see his family every day. And at night, he wanted to hold Jean, and have her hold him, when it was dark.

And yet, in another part of his mind, statistics suddenly fascinated him. He had roughly a thousand meals to eat; a couple of hundred bowel movements; maybe, ideally, four hundred orgasms to go, tops—

"Jeff, I don't know . . ." Jean said, unconsciously looking back at the house again, then at Griffin, who said nothing but smiled a lot. The idea of having only four hundred orgasms ahead of him had a strangely positive effect. Thinking about four hundred orgasms would cheer anybody up.

"Okay, okay," Jean said, "now, please just—"

"You'll do it?" Griffin said, happily. "Great! Look, from now on, I'll give you more space as a person—"

"Wait—"

"—and room to grow and your potentials and all that stuff."

"Hold it! I'll *think* about it! That's all! I'll think about it." She paused and thought about it. "The boys *would* love it . . ." Griffin was just about to excitedly agree, but she cut him off with a gesture.

"I've really got to get back inside, Jeff. I'll call you tomorrow. Okay?"

Griffin glanced toward the house, more aware than ever before that someone was inside. He looked back at Jean, his excitement about the trip now fading away.

"We're going to finally take that trip together, as a family," Griffin said, slowly, "and I gotta get out of here because you have a date. Is that it?"

Jean half-smiled and half-shrugged, hoping he would understand. He did, but he didn't like it. He turned to go, then stopped.

"Do the boys like him? Do they call him something cornball like Uncle Frank or whatever—"

"Jeff, for heaven's sake!"

Griffin instantly held his hand up, an immediate

24

gesture of surrender. He forced a smile. Jean went back inside.

Just then, Bobby, in the midst of a jump shot, yelled, " 'Bye, Dad!"

"Yeah, 'bye, Dad!"

Griffin turned to go over to join them but saw that they never let the game slow down for a second. He sort of half-waved, went back to his car, and drove away.

JANUARY-FEBRUARY, 1975—
SEATTLE

The chest X rays, the endless blood samples, the strange graphs made by strange medical machinery—all began to blur together in Sarah Phoenix's mind.

She went from doctor to specialist to medical teams and back again. She talked to tall doctors, short doctors, fat ones, and thin ones.

More than once, she stomped out, slamming doors behind her. The one thing that set her off was to sense a smugness among doctors that there was something that medical science just couldn't beat.

Only once did she get drunk.

A man at a bar came over and sat down beside her and smiled. He wore a polyester leisure-suit that was a color not found in nature, white shoes, and matching white belt.

"What's your name, honey?" he had cleverly said.

"Leukemia," she heard herself say. "Miss Leukemia Phoenix."

The man had stared at her.

"Like the disease?"

"Like the city," she said, and had gone home, alone.

What she lacked in cash in trying to reach medical experts, she made up for with sheer ingenuity. Being a legal secretary, she had friends check into any way in which she was eligible for free medical tests through state or national programs. She took advantage of every one. She had personally contacted specialists, trying to make her case sound like a challenge. She coaxed, pleaded, and threatened.

She made phone calls.

She made trips.

She sent telegrams.

She became a minor legend at a regional medical convention.

Phoenix simply couldn't understand why, in this day and age, she couldn't find one doctor who could do a simple thing like save her life.

Eventually, the final interviews with doctors became a boring routine.

"You couldn't have made some mistake?" asked Phoenix, knowing what each of them would say next.

"I'm sorry, no," said a young doctor, who felt terrible.

"And you can't come up with any treatments that will buy me any real time?"

"No."

"You can't save my life?"

"No."

"Can you validate my parking ticket?"

JANUARY, 1975—APPROACHING CALIFORNIA DESERT

At precisely 9 P.M., Griffin and his family were parked in the middle of a large trailer park, and Griffin was struggling in the middle of a large tent.

"Okay, Bobby, are you getting the main pole? Huh?" Griffin's muffled questions came from under the sagging canvas. "Jean, is the main tent peg lined up in front?"

He thought his family was helping him pitch the tent. They were, in fact, sitting on camping stools, without expression, watching him struggle. The only movement was that of the moths around the Coleman lantern. Even the dog looked bored. Griffin continued to be a moving shape under the big, heavy tent.

"Billy, you got the side straight yet?"

"Jeff, for heaven's sake, we don't have to *practice* this," Jean finally said. "We'll be in Yosemite tomorrow night and *then* we can put the tent up."

Griffin stuck his head out from under the tent.

"Yeah, but I thought it would be fun to do, you know, all of us together. Huh, guys?"

Griffin looked to his two sons for support. They didn't respond.

"Then when the tent's up," Griffin continued, like an overenthusiastic cruise director, "we can all learn the constellations . . ."

"Aw, Dad, constellations are *gross*." That was the twelve-year-old.

"Yeah, Dad, really *gross*." That was the eight-year-old.

"The camp director said we could watch his TV. Can't we, Dad? Please?" Both, together.

Griffin slowly emerged from under the tent. "Hey, fellows, we don't get that much time together—"

The eight-year-old instinctively turned away from his Saturday father. "Mom? Please?"

"Be back by ten," Jean said.

"We don't get that much time together, guys—" Griffin stepped toward them, but they were off and running, cheering, and the dog ran with them, barking.

Griffin started to call after them, reaching out, but then he stopped himself. Sighing, he left the tent and sat by his wife. It was quiet for a moment. Griffin turned to her.

"They'll be gone for hours," he leered. "Let's go in the camper. I'll show you my mosquito bites if you show me yours."

Jean just gave him a sour look.

Griffin looked away and found himself watching other families camped nearby. One family sat by the lantern, having a late dinner, with Mom serving some stew. Another young couple sat on their car hood, just talking. A large family was laughing as a baby was awkwardly walking among them.

Griffin turned to her, gesturing, speaking softly.

"Jean, if we could just *try* . . . it's getting late . . ."

Jean gave him a cold look; this whole trip had

27

turned out to be a terrible idea, and besides, she knew nine o'clock wasn't late.

Griffin saw she still had that fed-up look. His feelings were all over his face, and he had to turn away. When he looked back to quickly cover up, he leaped to his feet in a frustrated comic-rage.

"Okay," he said loudly. "So you don't think the great outdoors is so great, huh? Well, I'll tell you . . ." He began to unbutton his shirt. ". . . maybe you just gotta get in the spirit of the thing a little more."

She just stared at him. The next thing she knew, he had taken his shirt off, climbed up on a little rickety camping stool, begun pounding his chest, and given out the loudest, wackiest Tarzan yell ever heard.

"AHHH . . . eeeee . . . AHHHH!"

People started. Lights went on. Jean was dying of embarrassment, hissing at him to get down. That was all he needed. He gave out one more long yell, pounding his chest some more, having a fine time.

MARCH, 1975—
MONTEREY, CALIFORNIA

The drive south along Pacific Coast Highway is absolutely beautiful, even at eighty-five miles an hour, the way Phoenix drove it. Her three-year-old red VW never slowed down for the curves, even the ones beside the high cliffs.

With the ocean waves breaking on rocks far below, Phoenix passed a slower car—on the right, five feet from the edge of the cliff.

That put her in a good mood.

It was a terrific day. She had the window rolled down, and the wind messed up her hair. She loved it.

A station wagon up ahead was actually driving at the required 55 m.p.h. Phoenix saw the oncoming truck but passed the station wagon, on the left this time, and whipped back into the right lane, just in time. The diesel truck roared past the VW a second later, its horn sounding like the angry roar of a great beast.

The seafood restaurant, an hour later, was a little too nautical for Phoenix's taste, but it had windows overlooking the ocean. Phoenix spent more time looking at the restaurant than at the view, however. The decorator for the place, she decided, must have been Tugboat Annie. Fishnets hung everywhere, full of stuffed sailfish, starfish, blowfish, and the salt shakers were little boats. The restrooms, Phoenix thought to herself, were probably labeled "Inboards" and "Outboards."

She was about halfway through her dinner when the man came over to her table. She saw him coming and quickly realized that in another time she would have loved to see him heading her way. He was tall, tan, about thirty-five, wore a suede jacket, and had a friendly, sexy smile.

"Excuse me," the man said, "but I see you're eating by yourself." God, thought Phoenix, he's even got a sexy voice. "I am, too," he said, "except for this extremely boring book. Would you join me so I can stop reading it?"

Phoenix smiled, in spite of herself. The total approach, including the guy himself, got an eight on a scale from one to ten. Eights you don't get everyday.

"What's your book?"

"It's a fascinating, in-depth study . . . *The Complete History of Scissors.*"

She grinned and he grinned back.

"Yeah, I just finished a really moving book by the same author," Phoenix said. "It's called *Hitler Without Tears.*"

The man laughed.

"I was going to read that one," he said, "but I've been waiting for it to come out in hardback." He stopped grinning then and just looked at her. Her knees got a little weak. "Would you like to join me?"

Yeah, thought Phoenix, for the next fifty years.

"Thank you, but I have to be going soon," she said.

"Are you in that much of a hurry?"

"Yes," she said quietly. He knew she meant it. He

29

smiled and returned to his own table, graciously accepting what she said. Phoenix sighed to herself and looked at the ocean.

Back on the highway, her VW went screaming around a curve at a dangerous speed, past a sign that said "Los Angeles, 348 miles." She drove all night long, in a hurry, going nowhere.

JUNE, 1975—LOS ANGELES

The kite looked very pretty against the blue sky, but it kept losing altitude.

Griffin, wearing jeans and a sweatshirt, ran up and down the beach, tugging on the kite string, trying as hard as he could to keep the kite up in the air.

But the kite continued its down spiral in a crazy pattern just above the ocean waves and finally crashed into the sea.

Griffin started to make one last try to save it, but then could only stand, panting, watching it crash. He straightened up, felt disgusted with himself, then noticed that he had an audience.

Three old men sat on a bench. They all wore layers of clothes, even though it was a hot, sunny day. Such old men are as much a part of the Southern California beaches as seagulls and litter. Two of the old men were absorbed in a game of checkers, but the third, wearing a green scarf, had been watching Griffin try to get his kite up. He regarded Griffin rather sourly, not impressed by his efforts.

Griffin threw the ball of string into the ocean after the kite, then trudged through the sand to his apartment.

Griffin's apartment was cheap and not very new, but it was right on the beach. As he got closer, he noticed that a man in a suit and tie was sitting on his steps, waiting for him. Griffin recognized the man.

"George!" said Griffin, completely surprised. "How the hell—"

"How are you, Jeff?" George said, walking toward him.

"How did you find me?" Griffin made it a point not to let anyone know where he was until he was ready.

"Through Dr. Feinberg," George said, standing in front of his little brother. "How are you doing?"

At the question, the two men were quiet for a moment.

"If you talked to Feinberg," Griffin said softly, "you know how I'm doing."

The two men suddenly, awkwardly embraced.

JUNE, 1975—LOS ANGELES

Phoenix gazed out of the office window at the palm trees across the street. She still wasn't used to them yet.

"Why did you leave Seattle for Los Angeles?" asked the psychiatrist, in his usual serious manner.

"It rained during the day, and I cried a lot at night," Phoenix explained, "and I wanted to move to a drier climate." She realized that the palm trees all looked like upside-down phallic symbols to her. Better not mention that to a shrink, she decided. "Besides, I want to see Disneyland before I die."

The psychiatrist gestured a lot.

"But do you feel that this move was a running away *from* something, or a moving *toward* something?"

Phoenix glanced out of the window again, looking at a particularly big palm tree, and tried to keep a straight face. The psychiatrist looked sincere and intense.

She couldn't help it. She laughed.

"I'm sorry . . ." she said, trying to get serious, but failing, "suddenly this just all seems so absurd. I mean, what am I trying to do? Be the sanest, most well-adjusted, corpse in the cemetery?"

She smiled at the man and stood up, starting to leave.

"Thank you, doctor, but . . ."

31

She shrugged away the rest, and he smiled and nodded. He understood. His training was geared to preparing people for life, not death, and he wasn't all that sorry to see her go. As she opened the door, he wrote something on a card and handed it to her.

"Wait. An associate of mine is teaching an upper-level psychology course. Call him. I think he might let you in as a special-interest student."

He held the card out for her.

"What is it you think I might have a special interest in?" She took the card and looked a little surprised when she read the name of the class.

JUNE, 1975—LOS ANGELES

George was as easy to talk to as ever, as they sprawled around Griffin's apartment, having a beer.

"So what's new and exciting in the old home town?"

"Nothing much, I guess. Oh, remember Jerry Martin and his wife, Claudine? They hosted a consciousness-raising session for men on the women's movement," George said.

"That doesn't sound like Albuquerque, New Mexico."

"Well, the women only attended the very first session. Now, once a week, I bring beer, Smitty brings poker chips, and Robin Westlin usually brings some stag movies."

"That sounds like Albuquerque, New Mexico," Griffin said.

The two men smiled and sipped their beer. The hot afternoon sun came through the windows, and they were silent for a few moments.

"Jean's pretty worried," George finally said, quietly. "Have you called her?"

"I'd just hear outraged indignation at being left on the highway in the desert."

"That was five months ago. Now, she's just worried about *you*."

32

Griffin paced around the room, waving his arms as he spoke.

"What do I say? That I'm all right and she shouldn't worry? Well, I'm not all right. There's nothing to say anymore. That's why I left." Griffin paused, and then sat back down. "How are the boys?"

"Fine. Bobby's at baseball practice all day, and Billy announced last week he wants to become a doctor."

"I meant—"

"I know what you meant. Don't worry about them. You know kids. They're stronger than adults."

Griffin finished his beer, crushed the can in his hands, then tossed it in a high arc toward a toy basketball hoop he had nailed to the wall in the corner above the wastepaper basket. He missed.

"There's enough in my savings and that stock, isn't there?" Griffin asked.

George just smiled.

"You knew I'd be there to help Jean straighten everything out."

"Yeah," Griffin said. "I knew."

George reached into his jacket pocket and handed Griffin an envelope. "That reminds me. Here's $1500. There's more if—"

"Jean will need it," Griffin said, not touching it. "I'll manage."

"This isn't your money. It's what I saved. Take it. Fly to Paris for breakfast, I don't care what you do with it."

Griffin took the envelope and the two men looked a little embarrassed.

George finally relaxed. The rough parts were over. Brothers can talk to each other about just about anything comfortably, except each other's money and each other's families.

"So what the hell have you been doing, anyway?" George said, finishing his beer.

"Well, I decided that Los Angeles is a good place to finally get some things done. I've been body-surfing. Took a night course on writing a novel, but that didn't

33

work. Oh, and I finally went to a massage parlor. Always wanted to."

George looked up, inquisitively, having always wanted to go himself. Griffin shook his head. George shrugged.

"My problem is that there's only one thing I've got any real interest in," Griffin said, reaching for a nearby newspaper-like schedule of college courses. "And I see there's even a class in it . . ." He looked at the schedule.

Amid the long lists of classes, one had been circled: "PSY 458 Psychology of Death and Dying 7:30 MWF."

The college auditorium could have held over two hundred students, but only about two dozen had enrolled. The low enrollment probably wasn't due so much to the subject matter, or because it was a night class, as to the combination.

"Most of you are graduate students in psychology," said the serious, middle-aged professor, beginning the class exactly on time. "Some are in mortuary science. And I know that a few of you enrolled because you have relatives who are near death and are personally trying to readjust."

Griffin looked as serious and attentive as the rest of the class.

An elderly man in the front row slowly raised his hand, and, with simple dignity, said, "I am here because I am old and I am dying."

This caused a tense silence in the class.

"We are all dying, a little at a time every day," said the professor in a kind way, "and none of us are ready. I'm glad you're in the class."

The professor returned to organizing his notes for a moment, but the tension remained.

A second later, a tall, gangly student burst into the auditorium, looked around confused for a moment, obviously lost, then spoke to the nearest student.

"Is this Punic Wars I and II?" The voice was supposed to be quiet but carried throughout the class.

The nearest student shook his head, saying, "Psych 458, Death-and-Dying."

The student gave a nervous chuckle, realized he was serious, stared at the class like they were ghouls, then fled, fearing for his life.

Griffin couldn't stop grinning.

"In studying the psychology of dying," the professor said, going right on as if nothing had happened, "we will discuss grief, tension, fear, and anger."

The more Griffin tried not to laugh, the more he wanted to. He looked around to see who else was about to break up. But everyone else was completely serious, too scared of the subject to relax and smile.

Then, sitting close by, Griffin saw the only other person in the class who was also trying not to laugh.

Phoenix.

Chapter Three

Griffin and Phoenix each had to look the other way or burst out laughing. The professor continued seriously. "When a friend or loved one dies, sadness is not all that we feel. We also feel anger at the one who dies . . . for abandoning us."

The professor droned on. Just for the hell of it, Griffin forced himself to act serious, then leaned over to Phoenix.

"This is very serious, Miss . . ." Griffin whispered, with a straight face. "You shouldn't laugh at the Punic Wars, really."

This, of course, made it much harder on Phoenix. Griffin leaned back in his own seat, waited a few moments with perfect comic timing, then leaned back toward her.

"Lots of people died in the Punic Wars, you know . . . both I and II," Griffin whispered, nodding soberly. "Really . . . lots of Punics . . ."

Phoenix, red-faced, hand over her mouth, almost burst out laughing.

A little later, the professor announced a five-minute break, and Griffin was the first one out in the hallway. As the rest of the students filed out and went over to the vending machines, they were completely serious. Griffin wasn't.

He got a cup of coffee and a candy bar and sat down by himself on some stairs.

Phoenix emerged from the sea of serious faces, spotted Griffin, and walked over to him.

"Thanks a lot," she said. "I almost broke up."

Griffin's mouth was full of candy, so he just made an expansive gesture that was supposed to mean that she was welcome.

"How come the whole class wasn't laughing?" he said.

"Zombies. They're busy taking death very seriously."

"The lady beside me kept glaring at me," Griffin said. "She doesn't think I'm very serious."

"Good."

They looked at each other. Griffin sipped his coffee.

"You weren't any better," he said. "I'll bet you used to get in trouble when you were a little girl for giggling in church."

"I threw up once in the collection plate."

"I put poison ivy in my brother's swimming trunks once."

"I poured ketchup on my cat and told the baby-sitter it backed into the fan. Is the coffee here any good?"

"Yeah," Griffin said. "You want a cup?"

"No. Why are we having this strange conversation?"

"I don't know. You started it."

"No, I didn't."

"You came over here."

"You looked at me," Phoenix said, and they regarded each other. Griffin stood up, put his coffee down, and wadded up the candy wrapper.

"Look, I hate to eat and run," he said, "but after a class like that, I have to use the men's room . . ."

"What did your brother do?"

"What? Oh . . ." The question caught Griffin off guard, and he stared off, somewhere else for a moment, strangely serious. "He gave me $1500 . . ."

This last comment was puzzling to Phoenix, but not any more so than this man or the class or her life lately. She turned and started back into the classroom.

"Hey," Griffin said, calling after her. She stopped and looked at him. "Save me a seat."

She thought about it a moment, smiled, and nodded.

After the break, the rest of the class continued without any foolishness.

". . . and thus," the professor continued, "in the same way that no two people face life exactly alike, no two people die the same way, either.

"Another area we will study is that of death and children. We lie to children through euphemisms about three places: the bedroom, the bathroom, and the grave. When a relative dies, a child is often told that Grampa has 'gone away' instead of hearing the truth. Yet the child senses fear behind such evasions, and grows up to pass the same vague apprehensions about death on to *his* children . . ."

The class, as before, all sat together down near the front, with two exceptions. Griffin and Phoenix sat listening to the lecture halfway up the big auditorium, together but apart from the rest of the class.

The two of them were listening seriously, or so Phoenix thought, until Griffin turned to her, completely deadpan, with a cigarette sticking out of each ear.

"Excuse me, do you have a match?"

She managed to whisper one thing back before they both started laughing.

"You smoke too much."

The night was cool and clear as people poured out of the school. Griffin almost lost sight of Phoenix in the crowd. She was walking away toward the parking lot.

"Hey! Phoenix!"

She stopped and turned as Griffin ran and caught up with her.

"How did you know my name?" she asked.

"Those discussion-group name tags. Is that your name or your place?"

"My name."

"My name is—"

". . . Griffin," she finished for him, having obviously noted his name tag, too. They grinned at each other.

"Are you a student here?" Griffin asked.

"No, I'm the night janitor."

"I mean, you go to classes full-time, or what?"

"No, I just thought that one would be interesting. It wasn't. What were you doing there?"

"Nothing," Griffin said, too quickly. "I mean, I took another course in writing a novel, that's all."

"You're a writer?"

"No, I used to sell life insurance."

"And now you're trying to be a writer?"

"No, now I'm hungry," Griffin said. "I know a place that makes terrific tacos."

"I do, too," Phoenix said, walking away from him.

"Hey! Wait a minute!"

She stopped, a few feet away.

"Your beguiling charm and a terrific taco will not get you into my evening, my life . . . or anywhere else." She continued to walk away.

Suddenly, Griffin was at her side; he grabbed her by the elbow and spun her around. He wasn't smiling any more.

"Look, don't flatter yourself. My life's a little complicated right now."

"So's mine."

"Fine. We understand each other. Now I'm going to tell you when and where I'll be eating dinner Wednesday night. You can show up or not, I don't care."

They glared at each other, stubbornly.

Griffin sat in a window booth of a restaurant, waiting. He had been there twenty minutes.

Across the street, at an ice cream parlor, Phoenix watched Griffin. She knew he was twenty minutes late.

Phoenix watched the side of his head through the blur of rush-hour traffic that blocked her line of vision. He never once turned and looked in her direction.

She sipped her coffee, feeling childish. Monday night, after meeting Griffin, she was positive she'd never meet him for dinner, remembering how gruff he'd gotten after class.

Tuesday morning, when she woke up, remembering his gruffness felt good to her so she decided to show up after all. By Tuesday night, she recalled how strange he had acted, and decided to forget it.

Wednesday morning, while staring into her closet,

she decided the matter had now been taken out of her hands. After all, she didn't have anything new and . . . well . . . interesting to wear.

Wednesday afternoon, she went shopping.

Griffin sat waiting, in a trusting way.

Phoenix felt guilty about not going across the street, but knew if anything came of their date, she'd feel a lot guiltier later.

Then again, it was not an actual date. She never said she'd meet him. There you go again, she thought to herself.

She hated being indecisive, like her mother. Her mother was the kind of person who, when faced with any decision, didn't know whether to shit or wind her watch.

At that moment, Griffin slowly turned, looked right at her from across the street, tilted his head, stuck his tongue out, and crossed his eyes.

Flustered at being caught, she was now forced to go across the street, to save face.

She paid for her coffee, marched across the street and into the restaurant, feeling foolish. She walked right up to the booth where Griffin was sitting and sat across from him. He smiled at her, but didn't move.

"Don't get up," she said.

"You look pretty when you're hostile."

"And stop looking so pleased with yourself."

"You know what we're going to do tonight?"

"Don't tell me what we're going to do tonight," Phoenix said, irritated and confused. "I don't even know you, and you're a very strange person, and I don't know what I'm doing here in the first place."

"Tonight," Griffin said, going right on as though she hadn't said a word, "we're going to eat dinner and cut class, then we're going to do something you've secretly always wanted to do, but never really had the nerve."

The last time she had heard that, she was a freshman in college, and was in the back seat of a '57 Chevy. But she was as curious now as she had been then.

"What?"

"Sneak in to a movie through the exit doors."

41

"I've got money to buy a ticket."

"I have, too."

They were very quiet as they crept down the alley beside the movie theater, past some trash barrels, then down a small stairway that led to the exit door.

"What if we get caught?" Phoenix whispered.

"In this state," Griffin said, "it's the chair."

It was dark and quiet. Griffin tried the door. It was open, but creaked a little.

"Once I open it, step through quickly, then sit down right away," he said.

She nodded.

Griffin opened the heavy exit door and the sound-track from the movie inside got louder. The door creaked.

About thirty feet away, a big kid about twenty in an usher's outfit that didn't fet too well turned at the creaking sound.

He saw two silhouettes slip in and quickly take the two nearest seats.

Not amused, the usher took out his flashlight and started toward them.

As they sat down, Griffin glanced up at the screen, where screaming brown natives were fleeing molten lava from a volcano.

"Picked up the plot yet?" he whispered to Phoenix.

"I need some Milk Duds. Could you steal me some?"

"No way, lady."

"You've got to. I can't enjoy a movie unless—"

The usher's flashlight hit their faces, and his hand was on Griffin's shoulder.

"Excuse me, sir," the kid said sarcastically, "but would you both come to the manager's office with me?"

"Uh, yeah, sure," Griffin said. He and Phoenix got up. "Milk Duds . . ." Griffin mumbled, under his breath.

They headed up the aisle, first the usher, then Phoenix, then Griffin, who suddenly remembered the advice from an old Army training film about being captured behind enemy lines. The best time to escape was immediately after capture, when you had the fewest people guarding you, and were still near friendly territory.

He quietly tapped Phoenix on the shoulder, and the two of them silently turned and hurried back down the aisle toward the exit door.

When the usher turned and yelled at them, they broke into a run, bursting through the exit doors. Griffin leaped up the stairs three at a time, then ran on past the trash barrels. Phoenix was right behind him, but paused long enough to shove the trash cans down the stairs, just as the big usher, angry as hell, came charging out.

The barrels clanked loudly down the stairs, right into the shins of the usher, who fell over them, yelling things about Griffin's recent ancestry.

Laughing, Griffin and Phoenix disappeared around the corner of the alley, running as fast as they could.

They ran an extra two blocks, then leaned against a building, completely exhausted.

They went window-shopping, staring in dark stores.

They stopped and bought a giant-sized, sloppy pizza, but, as they walked along, didn't get very much into their mouths.

Griffin had to talk Phoenix out of hitchhiking to Pasadena.

Phoenix had to talk Griffin out of climbing the fence at the La Brea tar pits and riding the mastodon.

They stopped in front of a drugstore and Phoenix decided she wanted to get her picture taken in a 25¢ photo booth. She took a long time in front of a mirror, getting her hair just right, then seated herself inside and closed the little curtain. She waited a few seconds, for the first of four little green lights that signal that a picture is being taken.

When she was comfortable and ready and smiling, Griffin decided he wanted his picture taken and charged through the curtain, landing on Phoenix's lap. She tried to shove him out. During the battle, which created a lot of yelling and almost made the photo booth rock back and forth, the machine indifferently took its four required pictures. By the time the pictures emerged, they were gone.

They were walking down a side street, an hour later, when they saw a kid siphoning gas from a car a hundred yards away.

"Crime in the streets," said Griffin. "A result of economic pressure and subsequent moral decay."

The teen-age kid was big and wore a T-shirt to show off his muscles, but he nervously glanced around, quickly trying to finish.

Phoenix started to head in the other direction, but Griffin, with a strange smile on his face, took her by the elbow and steered her directly toward the kid.

Phoenix didn't know what the hell was going on, but didn't ask; most of the time, with Griffin, she didn't know what the hell was going on.

"Okay, kid! Stand up! Hands on the car!" Griffin ran around the front of the car, startling the kid, screaming like a banshee and waving his arms. "C'mon, spread 'em! Let's go! NOW!"

The terrified kid quickly assumed the frisking position, hands on the car, leaning forward, legs spread. Griffin looked at Phoenix, unsure for a second, then yelled some more as he awkwardly frisked the kid, patting his sides and legs. "C'mon, let's go, spread 'em!"

Griffin wasn't sure what to do next.

"Now," he said, trying to sound official, "Sergeant Flagstaff wil read you your rights. Sergeant?"

Phoenix was caught totally off guard.

"Uh, yeah, okay . . . you have the right to remain silent. You have the right to have an attorney present . . . uh . . ." She'd watched a lot of television, but not *that* much.

"You've got the right to have a doctor present . . ." Griffin said, coming to the rescue. ". . . and we have the right to have a judge present or something. Now, kid," he said, "you're in a lot of trouble! This is it! You got a mother?"

"Huh?" the kid said. This was the weirdest cop he'd ever been busted by. "What?"

"I asked you if you got a mother!" Griffin screamed.

"Yeah! Yeah, I do!"

Griffin leaned close and tried to look mean.

"Do you think she'd be proud of you right now?"

Phoenix stared off down the street so the kid wouldn't see her trying not to laugh.

"Go on, get out of here," Griffin said, acting disgusted with him. "I'm letting you off this time. *But watch it!*"

Unsure, the kid looked around for a second.

"Beat it!" Griffin yelled.

"Thanks, man, no shit," the kid mumbled, and ran off down the street. Phoenix shook her head to herself, smiling at Griffin, who put on his sincere face.

"This moment," intoned Griffin, to the world in general, trying to sound profound, "has been the turning point in that boy's life, and he will now become a fine person."

Phoenix smiled in amazement at Griffin and said, "I wouldn't be surprised."

It was 4 A.M. and the big parking lot by the Santa Monica beach was empty except for two people. Dawn was still just sort of a pencil sketch somewhere, not yet ready for actual production.

"Watching the sunrise is a beautiful idea, Griffin," said Phoenix, "but I'm tellin' ya, it usually comes up in the east."

"Well," said Griffin, "you never know."

They each were resting on the hoods of their respective cars, leaning back against the windshields. The cars were parked side by side, angled a little toward each other, facing a dull green sea and dark gray sky.

They each held a styrofoam cup of steaming coffee. The wind was cool in the early morning hours. They sipped their coffee and watched the western horizon, waiting for the sun to come up. It was a comfortable silence, and they were tired from walking around all night. The problem was, the night was about over.

Phoenix finally spoke.

"I've had more fun with you tonight than I've had in months."

"I've had more fun with me tonight than I've had in months, too," Griffin said.

"And if I didn't think I'd start to like you so much, I'd probably see you again."

"What?"

"I still don't know a damn thing about you," Phoenix said, "except that you're just crazy enough that, well . . . I just can't get involved with anyone right now."

"Who said anything about getting involved?"

Phoenix was embarrassed.

"Oh. I guess I'm flattering myself again, aren't I? I shouldn't have assumed . . . oh, I'm just babbling . . ." She was quiet a moment. "Did you ever not want a new day to start?"

"Why do you think we're looking in this direction?" Griffin said softly.

Phoenix looked at him and realized it was the first time he had ever actually been serious.

Griffin dropped his eyes and made a big thing out of sipping his coffee, and Phoenix watched a seagull.

Then she suddenly got down off her car hood and handed her cup of coffee to Griffin.

"Here, there's still some left. I gotta go," she said, suddenly getting in her car. "Thanks for the night. Take care of yourself. You're quite a guy."

She started her car as Griffin, mildly stunned by all this and still holding the two cups of coffee, instinctively began to stop her.

"Hey . . ."

She looked up at him, waiting.

One thought kept going through his mind: I have no right to ask her to stay.

"Don't . . ." he mumbled, confused, until all he could say was, ". . . don't you want your coffee?"

Phoenix shook her head, put the car in gear, and tore out of the empty gray parking lot. Griffin just stood there, watching her leave. He let the two cups of coffee slide through his fingers.

Phoenix tore along the freeway in the predawn dimness. She suddenly cut in between two cars. Both honked at her.

Chapter Four

JULY, 1975—LOS ANGELES

The sight of Griffin trying to run through sand would have been comical, except that he was trying very hard to get the kite in the air.

The kite danced around just above the waves but lost altitude and settled into the sea, not even making a splash.

Griffin stopped running, defeated. He noticed the same old man with the green scarf. The old man was walking on the beach nearby, slowly shaking his head to himself at Griffin's futile efforts.

Griffin trudged back through the sand to his apartment and forced himself to begin a letter he'd been avoiding.

The old typewriter did its best to pound out the message but somehow it didn't look right:

My Sons,
    I am leaving this for you to read after I am gone. Forgive me for not being around you more during my last year, but someday you will understand

Griffin stopped typing after the word "understand." When he was a kid, he hated it whenever people told him that "someday" he would understand something.

Hell, he still didn't understand. And something told him that if you spot-checked with a dozen oldtimers, *they* still didn't understand.

Angrily, Griffin gave up. He tore the sheet out of the typewriter, wadded up the paper, and tossed it toward his basketball hoop over the wastebasket. He missed.

He got up and wandered around his apartment for a few minutes, bored, restless, feeling guilty that he didn't finish the letter. It had been such a good idea, to leave something they could read from him on their 21st birthday or something, some really personal father-to-son message, one that might even help them someday. He decided it was still a good idea and would try it again after taking a break. He turned on the television and watched pro football.

Griffin never tried to write the letter again. He decided that if his sons ever wondered why he never left them some special letter that answered their questions and articulated his feelings about life, well, someday they would understand.

Phoenix considered herself somewhat of an expert on the décor in doctors' offices. She felt more comfortable in the stark, cold-looking ones than in the pseudo-homey offices like this one.

"I appreciate the fact that you have done some reading on the subject," a tall doctor was saying, "but chemotherapy would only be temporarily helpful in your case."

"What about radiation therapy?" she asked.

The doctor smiled to himself. He wasn't used to patients who did so much homework.

"I'm sorry, but your disease is too widespread. In fact, it might even do you more harm than good."

"I just thought that . . . maybe . . ."

He leaned close, and spoke to her gently.

"If you know enough to ask the questions, you must know the answers."

She just sat there, wondering how much he had paid for his antique rolltop desk.

Griffin finally figured out what had gone wrong with

his marriage one day while sitting on the side of an L.A. freeway, waiting for a tow truck, and glaring at a flat tire.

It wasn't the place he would have picked to finally think things out and stumble across a few insights. But then, it wasn't even the place he would have picked to have a flat tire.

Griffin had been twenty-four when he and Jean had met and gotten married. She was twenty-two, beautiful, and full of life. It was 1962, the last of the great years.

Actually, Jean had been the second girl Griffin falled in loved with. The first time was when he had just turned eighteen. There was a girl with red hair, a high, squeaky voice, and not much of a figure, and Griffin had the biggest case of puppy love for her anyone could ever have. It was his freshman year at college and she was all he thought about all year, even though he could rarely get a date with her.

During his sophomore year, Griffn's fraternity brothers were getting pinned and engaged, right and left. They were dropping like flies. Griffin thought it was stupid to make permanent commitments like that at age 18 or 19. How was a man supposed to know who else he might meet, or what career possibilities he might miss out on because he couldn't take some chances, because of premature responsibilities?

Griffin actually thought like that in those days. He really did.

As a result, Griffin never really seriously went after the skinny girl with the red hair (not that he would have known how, anyway) and she faded out of his life before she ever knew how important she had been to him.

Griffin played it smart. He graduated from college free of commitments.

He worked very hard, learning life insurance sales, and two years later, when he met Jean, he was a hard-charging, successful young man. People always said of him that he was doing very well. Griffin had enjoyed being a bachelor, but was now in the mood to settle down. Getting married at that point in his life seemed right.

It wasn't that Griffin didn't love Jean. He had felt nervous and excited about kissing her the first time, and three weeks later, while half-falling off his sofa while a scratchy Kingston Trio record played, his hands actually trembled the first time he unhooked her bra. (They made no further sexual progress that night: it was 1962, and in those days *You Waited*.) Griffin even loved her the day he swore as much to God and the state of New Mexico.

Griffin and his bride honeymooned in Las Vegas and never once did any gambling or saw any of the shows. Bobby was born a year later, Billy four years later, and Griffin worked harder than ever and became the best life insurance salesman in the region. They bought a small house and a large dog. They saved their money and someday hoped to buy a large house and a small dog.

Griffin now looked back on the thirteen years of his marriage the way Time was shown passing in old movies, where calendar pages rapidly fell away, or when a tree limb outside a window quickly changed from having little buds in spring, to autumn leaves, to snow. Somewhere between the green leaves of summer and the icicles, Griffin and Jean had lost something.

In subtle ways, over the years, Jean seemed to change, to harden. She once used to love to go to carnivals to ride the roller coaster, but once the boys were big enough, Griffin aways took them without her. Jean had majored in art history, and Griffin used to admire her knowledge and love of paintings. But Jean hadn't been near a museum in the last ten years. Griffin secretly wondered if Jean wasn't just mad that she couldn't stay twenty-two all her life, but it was probably more than that. He knew Jean wasn't a bad person and was always sorry that he never understood what had soured her on life over the years. It was funny that he never thought to just ask her.

Griffin did realize there were two very unfair, irrational things he'd always hold against Jean. The first was simply that universal blame that, somehow, it's your spouse's personal fault because your own life didn't turn out to be special and exciting. And Griffin knew that some small, childish part of him would always be a little mad at Jean just because she wasn't the skinny girl with red hair from a million years ago.

He and Jean loved each other out of habit over the last four or five years of their marriage, their passion just good enough to link together one predictable chunk of time with another.

Then, one day, they had looked at each other and it took each of them a long, terrible second to remember why they had gotten married. Without a sound, during that one moment, the last bond between them silently separated, the final strand from a torn cobweb.

Loud arguing and cliché rhetoric followed, of course, as though to cover up the sad, simple parting of two people. Extraneous issues were dragged in, accusations made, old hurts resurrected, and other parrying and thrusting. None of the noise would have wrecked a healthy marriage, but theirs was rotten underneath, where you couldn't see it. They each agreed to a trial separation, and they each knew they'd never get back together. But getting a divorce can take almost as much energy as making a marriage work, so things just drifted until last January when Griffin privately found out his occasional chest pains would stop in about a year, forever.

The tow-truck driver arrived and hauled Griffin and his car to a service station. The driver was mercifully quiet, leaving Griffin to his confused thoughts.

One thing, unfortunately, was clear.

He had loved and married Jean too much from his head, and not enough from his gut.

Women blurred together in his mind . . . the girl with red hair . . . Jean at twenty-two . . . Jean at thirty-five . . . and now Phoenix. No wonder he hesitated about her. It wasn't even just the small detail that he'd be dead soon.

With his track record, he'd be gun-shy about women if he was going to live a thousand years. But, of course, he wasn't. He would only live long enough to see a last awkward chapter in the story of Jeff and Jean, two crazy kids who got married and lived happily never after.

At the service station, a mechanic kept chattering away, and Griffin was forced to return to the present.

"Let's see . . ." the mechanic said, flipping through a thick catalogue with greasy fingers. "Okay, your Dunlop 125, 855 by 14 full-ply radial, steel-belted tire will run you . . . $54.76."

"What!" Griffin said. "Fifty-four bucks for a tire!"

"Well, you know, the rubber shortage."

"What rubber shortage?"

"Look, I can slap a temporary patch on that tire you got there," the mechanic said, pointing to Griffin's tire, now wedged around a circular steel disk, awaiting repair. "It's still got some good tread, and might last you a year, but you'll keep getting flats . . ."

"If it'll last a year, I'll take it," Griffin said, wryly.

Phoenix finally remembered Jody's husband's first name and grabbed the phone book. It was one of those funny, hard-to-remember names. Tom.

Phoenix quickly dialed the number.

"Hello?"

"Jody? Hey! It's Sarah!"

"Oh, no! Phoenix! Is that you?"

"Jody! Hey!"

They laughed, happy and excited. They had only seen each other twice in the ten years since college. They were always living in opposite parts of the country.

"How the hell are you?" Phoenix yelled.

"Up to my ass in kids!" Jody yelled back.

They laughed again. It was an old joke of theirs about children. During late-night discussions during their sophomore year, when every discussion is intense, every subject profound, Jody always said she wanted to wait eight or ten years before getting married and having children. Jody got married her junior year and was pregnant at graduation.

Phoenix always said she'd honestly like to have a family right away, if the right man came along. He didn't.

"Where *are* you? Still in Seattle?"

"No, I just moved to L.A.," Phoenix said. "Can I come over and—"

"What! You just moved here! Phoenix, we're moving to Boston right away!"

"Oh, no! I just got here! Can I come over? I haven't even seen the new one yet—"

"Phoenix, my whole house is upside-down today. There's cardboard boxes, and crap, and it's a mess—"

"Hey, I've seen cardboard boxes before," Phoenix said lightly, not realizing how tightly she was gripping the phone. Hearing a friendly voice was even more important to her than she had realized.

"Oh, it's a mess this week, Sarah. Listen, let's have lunch before we move, you know I want to see you."

"I've got the address and I can be there in a second —really, Jody, I'd love to see you and the kids."

Phoenix had nothing else to do that day. Boy, did she have nothing else to do.

"I want to see you, too, just to see if you've gained eight pounds like I have," Jody said, laughing, "but I know you haven't. But, really, Sarah, next week sometime would be better—"

Phoenix's voice had a strange tone to it that Jody had never heard before.

"C'mon, Jody . . . *please*?"

Griffin enjoyed wandering around the beach during the day, just watching people.

There were the muscle men, who publicly lifted weights as though they didn't know anyone was watching them.

There were the hard-core volleyball players who never smiled and made a religion out of it.

There were the thousands of attractive women who self-consciously undid the back of their bikini tops when they lay on their stomachs, hoping that a completely tan back might just make the difference.

Then there were the little kids who arranged globs of sand near the water. No wonder kids grew up confused, Griffin thought. When they play in the dirt at home, they catch hell, then they're dragged off to the beach and told to go play in the sand.

God only knows what the kids thought they were making, Griffin thought, certainly not castles. Songwriters came up with that nonsense. To the kids, they were just terrific big globs of wet sand.

One little girl, about five, flagrantly wearing a topless bathing suit, concentrated as she carefully poked holes into a pile of wet sand, using a stubby little finger which was attached to her bored, three-year-old brother. Trust was written on his face; he was proud to be a mere instrument in the hands of an artist.

Griffin went over to a hamburger stand and bought a hot dog and an orange drink. He turned to watch the kids in the distance, accidentally crashing into an absolutely beautiful young woman in a string bikini.

"Oops! Excuse me . . ."

"That's okay," said the girl, smiling. "I've seen you on the beach before, haven't I?"

"Yeah," Griffin said. Pretty snappy comeback, he thought. Gonna sweep her off her goddam feet any moment now.

"What sign are you?" she asked.

"Stegosaurus," he said, thinking about the tremendous difference between a regular bikini and a string bikini.

"Want to know what sign I am?" she asked with her same pretty smile.

"Sure."

"Cancer," she said, brightly.

Griffin looked at her, wondering why it was he thought she was so pretty. A two-week diet and a nose job wouldn't hurt her a bit, he decided, walking away.

Jody's living room was, in fact, full of cardboard boxes, but Phoenix was looking at a cute little one-year-old baby in a playpen in the corner.

"Jody, she's absolutely beautiful," Phoenix said.

"Yeah, she's okay," Jody said, with mock modesty. Jody was a fast-talking, attractive woman with blond hair. At the moment, her hair was in a scarf. She wore a sweatshirt and jeans, and was packing dishes into a box.

Six-year-old Tommy burst into the living room, slamming the door behind him.

"Mommy," Tommy hollered, "Jennifer's sitting in the dirt!"

Jody rolled her eyes toward Phoenix.

"He's going through that difficult stage for boys," she said quietly, "you know, from ages three to thirty-eight." Then she smiled at the boy.

"Tommy, do you remember Sarah? You were just Jennifer's age the last time she visited us."

"Hi, Tommy," Phoenix said.

Before their eyes, Tommy changed from the hard-charging man who could make loud announcements to a little boy, hit by an instant attack of shyness. His eyes on the carpet, he began to twist off a shirt button for poise.

Jody stood up.

"You want some more coffee before I go play Super-Mom?" Phoenix shook her head, so Jody went out the front door, yelling, "Jennifer! Stay out of the mud!" The screen door slammed behind her.

Phoenix looked at Tommy. He had blond hair and green eyes and wore red tennis shoes, blue jeans, and a T-shirt that said in Old English lettering, "I'm the reason Mom can't cope."

Phoenix leaned closer to him.

"Do you like your new baby sister?"

"No," Tommy said blandly.

At what age do they learn the secret, Phoenix wondered. By nine years old, he would instinctively know that when company asks something like that, you say "Yes." That means that somewhere between six and nine, they learn that lying really isn't bad, that it's good.

Jody came back in carrying three-year-old Jennifer, who was a little muddy around the edges. As she marched through, without pausing, she just said, "Sorry, gotta clean up her act."

"Sure," Phoenix said, then turned back to Tommy. "With all that curly hair, I'll bet you've got a lot of girl friends."

This was too much for Tommy. He hit the screen door at a dead run and was twenty feet away by the time it banged shut.

It was quiet, until the sound of a happy little gurgle made Phoenix turn.

The baby girl stood up in her playpen. She was wearing those flannel sleeper pajamas with feet on them, soft and white, with little elephants all over.

The baby looked at Phoenix and gurgled again.

There was a lot of smile, some drool on her chin, and two huge eyes that missed exactly nothing. She gave the side of the playpen a tiny little shake.

Phoenix got up from the sofa and went over to the playpen.

In the momentary quiet of the room, she slowly picked the baby up, gently, so very carefully, then hugged it like it was the most important thing in the world. She just stood there swaying a little from side to side. Phoenix kissed the baby and hugged it, but could not tell if she was imagining it or if the baby's little arms were actually trying to squeeze her back.

Phoenix heard Jody bustling around in the other room, so she made herself put the baby back in the playpen, just as Jody came back into the room, chattering away.

"Tom was so funny," Jody said. "Before we had kids, he couldn't wait to have a boy . . ."

She returned to packing dishes, not noticing that Phoenix had turned away from her, touching the edge of her eyes.

". . . but once we had both a boy and a girl, guess which one he fussed over the most?" Jody's shoulders slumped a little. In a resigned way, she said, "The boy."

She looked up at Phoenix, who then turned back around, forcing a smile.

"Hey! You've hardly said a thing about yourself," Jody said. "Come on, Phoenix, talk to me. What's new?"

Phoenix just smiled and shrugged, like there was nothing much new with her, and went over to help Jody pack dishes.

An hour later, on the front steps, Jody held the baby and Phoenix gave them both quick kisses.

"Write me when you get settled in Boston," Phoenix said.

"God, Sarah, it was so good seeing you!"

"You, too, Jody. My love to Tom." Phoenix started to go, then turned around and looked back. "You got a pretty nice family, you know."

Jody smiled and gestured away the compliment, and Phoenix walked away, waving, as Jody stepped back inside and closed the door.

Phoenix paused and looked back again before walking on down the sidewalk of the quiet suburban neighborhood. Her footsteps sounded unusually loud as she made the long walk to her car a few feet away.

It was one of those cool beach evenings, where everything was gray: the sea, the sky, the mood. The wind was cool, carrying the soothing sound of distant two-tone foghorns about every ten seconds.

Griffin got a good book, walked down to a local restaurant, had a quiet dinner, and slowly, deliberately, walked back. He liked listening to the foghorns, and he liked the cold sea air.

Inside his apartment, it was warm and cozy, and he peered out into the gray night. There was a single light from a single boat on the dark horizon. Griffin decided it was the perfect moment for a beautiful, loving woman to appear and enjoy the evening with him, but one didn't show up, so he watched TV a while and read before going to sleep.

Chapter Five

So far, the big Southern California amusement parks hadn't been amusing, but Phoenix kept trying them all, anyway.

Magic Mountain, after she'd been there about forty-five minutes, wasn't all that magic, either. The same kids, the same rides, the same Iowa license plates.

When it came to the big-scale rides and laughter the L.A. parks were famous for, Phoenix had become a fun junkie, hitting each one, hoping for a high she had never reached. Today, she sat on a bench, staring at the Magic Mountain waterfall, thinking back on the last few weeks.

Knott's Berry Farm was a real thrill, she thought to herself, remembering the hot afternoon she had sat around watching the picnic tables warp.

At Marineland, after three porpoises had not quite jumped through three hoops together, the happy voice over the loudspeaker had said, "How about that, folks! Wasn't that the greatest thing you've ever seen in your life?" While everyone else in the bleachers had applauded, Phoenix, sitting by herself, had said to herself, "No."

Phoenix got almost as sleepy as the sleeping animals when she drove through Lion Country Safari, and the Universal Studio tour was all right, except for when she was slowly herded through a replica of an exact model of Lucille Ball's dressing room.

Disneyland had been her favorite, until she saw a sign, bordered by little spaceships.

TOMORROWLAND! Inventions of the future! Each will become possible *in your lifetime!*

Phoenix had quickly gotten in line for the next free exhibit, to take her mind off what Disney thought was possible in her lifetime.

The next thing she knew, she was strapped into a stylized little bucket seat, attached to a conveyor belt, and found herself being taken into a series of darkened rooms. Realistic special effects and an announcer's taped voice told people taking the ride that "they were shrinking and on a journey through the marvels of the human body!"

Phoenix wanted out at that point.

It was too late.

A series of whirling lights flashed by her, as the announcer would periodically tell them they were now as small as a molecule, then an atom, meanwhile praising the miraculous mechanism of the human body.

As her seat spun around, through the darkness, Phoenix had been suddenly confronted by a twenty-foot, pulsating, healthy human cell, in living color. As Phoenix was hurled farther into the darkness of the surrealistic body, she heard the dull, steady, throbbing sound of a gigantic heart that was supposed to be growing closer on their fantasy journey.

The taped voice announced how many times a day this miraculous organ pumped life-giving blood through the body, and explained how antibodies are always in the bloodstream, waiting to attack harmful invaders. As the pounding increased, almost reverberating through her skull, Phoenix glanced up and saw a giant replica of the end of a twenty-foot microscope aimed at her. Through it, high above, was a realistic three-foot replica of a human eye, staring down at her.

The pounding continued.

The giant eye slowly blinked.

Phoenix had screamed.

She stared at the waterfall some more, rubbed her tired feet, and decided to try the famous Magic Mountain log ride. She waded through the crowd, looking more resigned than happy, until she smiled, suddenly recognizing someone through the exhibits and confusion.

Griffin.

He sat at a snack-bar patio in the middle of a million people, all of whom were frantically stuffing themselves with hamburgers and french fries.

He was alone, and bored.

A little boy about six ran up to him with a note.

Griffin smiled, took the note, and started to ask something, but the little boy ran off, disappearing into the crowd.

Confused, Griffin read the note: DID YOU SNEAK IN?

It wasn't signed. It didn't have to be.

He looked up. Then behind him. Everywhere.

But he didn't see her.

He quickly started to go one way, then another, peering into the crowd and the exhibits, running back and forth, searching everywhere.

He began to panic. He ran out of the snack-bar patio area. Now there were ten million faces, none of them the one he wanted to find.

Then a balloon man walked by, and as the beautiful balloons floated past, there was Phoenix.

She grinned at him, looking quite pleased with herself.

He started to shake his finger at her, but couldn't keep the happy grin off his face.

She had chosen to say hello to him, and he had wanted very much to find her. These two things were obvious to both of them as Griffin walked toward her.

Neither said anything. They were both just glad to see the other.

In a natural, almost routine way, Griffin simply took Phoenix by the arm and steered her toward some of the rides. Smiling, she left herself be taken away and they soon disappeared into the crowd.

Later that evening, on the special train that took them high above the park, Phoenix was finishing a story.

". . . anyway, so the only exciting thing that happened to me at Disneyland, really, was when one of Snow White's dwarfs tried to pick me up."

"Which one? Donner or Blintzen?"

"I thought it was Sneezy, but he said his name was Horny. He said he was Snow White's favorite," she said. "Hey, I've been doing all the talking. What about you? Been going to class, or what?"

"No, I transferred into Punic Wars I and II."

"Yeah, right," she said dryly. "And I'm in a new geography course, Turkey at the Crossroads. Griffin, what are you doing *here,* anyway?"

"Oh, I thought I might buy the place," Griffin said, gesturing broadly. "I've been thinking about tearing it down, maybe putting up a giant amusement park."

"Griffin, seriously, why did you—"

"Seriously? *Seriously?*" Griffin couldn't believe his ears.

"Sorry. Didn't mean to use that kind of language. Let's get off this silly train. I'll treat," she said. "You want cotton candy or a balloon?"

"Cotton candy. Balloons taste terrible."

They rode the famous log ride and when it hit the water, with a huge splash, they screamed louder than the kids.

They bought all fourteen of a man's helium balloons and then let them go, watching them slowly sail up and away.

They joined the delighted people watching the glass-blowing exhibit as an artist with glass and fire made an exquisite little winged horse.

Phoenix watched Griffin when he was looking in another direction. You did it again, Griffin, Phoenix thought to herself. I'm really enjoying myself.

Griffin's apartment looked even grubbier than usual when he and Phoenix entered that night.

"This afternoon," he said, hurriedly tossing some clothes in a closet out of sight, "I decided either to go

62

to an amusement park or clean up my apartment."

Phoenix could see dirty dishes, newspapers on the floor, and a shirt tossed over a chair.

"So which did you decide to do?"

"Sit down," Griffin said, still bustling around a little. "Let me get you a glass of cheap wine."

Phoenix continued to look around at the beat-up TV, a homemade desk, an old comfortable chair, and a funky makeshift bookcase.

"You've got everything but the poster of Steve McQueen on a motorcycle," she said.

"What?" yelled Griffin. He was around the corner in a little kitchenette area, quickly trying to wash two glasses.

"Nothing," she said, wandering around.

On a shelf, she saw a small, permanently sealed jar with the tiny grayish-green body of a baby octopus or squid preserved in a formaldehyde solution. The stiff, dead body, with clearly visible tentacles and suction cups, was disgusting.

"Ugh. Griffin, what *is* this thing?"

"What?" He stuck his head in. "Oh. That's my appendix. They'll let you keep them afterwards if you ask." He returned to his dishwashing.

Sufficiently revolted, she put it back and continued looking around the room, past some broken kites, to a small, cheap goldfish bowl. A couple of fish were alive, but the water needed changing and there was some green slime in there, too.

"I've got some goldfish, too," Phoenix said, leaning close, studying the slime. "Hey, I'm not a veterinarian or anything, but I think yours have hoof 'n' mouth disease. Now, you've got to bulldoze a big pit, you know, and herd them all in, and then—"

"What?" Griffin yelled from the next room.

"Nothing," she said, wandering around some more.

She dug into her purse and took out a small, beautiful little glass animal they had bought at the park. Griffin had held it up to the sunlight and announced that Life Was Like a Glass-Blown Winged Horse. When she asked him why, he said he had no idea, how was he supposed to know, and did she or did she not want an ice-cream bar.

Griffin came in with two glasses of wine, as Phoenix smiled and held up the beautiful little animal.

Griffin smiled, too. It was something they had both carefully picked out together, and he was glad Phoenix had remembered it.

"Where do you want this?" she said.

Griffin took it and studied a nearby shelf.

"I don't know . . . how about right here?"

They looked at it on the shelf.

"I think it would look better up here," she said, putting his appendix down below and the winged horse up front.

"You're right," Griffin said, "that's where it belongs."

She nodded in agreement, sipping her wine.

The moment the only thing they had in common was taken care of, a strange awkwardness began as they looked at each other again, not sure what came next. Griffin sat on the sofa and Phoenix sat in the chair and the space between them suddenly seemed wider than it really was.

Stalling, each sipped more wine and it was quiet in the room.

"So what part of this crazy town do you live in—"

"Hey, I don't need a stilted conversation. What the hell am I doing here, anyway?"

"How come you're so uncomfortable?"

She had no answer she could tell him and just got up and paced around for a minute. She wanted to be curled up next to him and out of the apartment for good, all at the same time.

"Have you ever noticed how we never ask each other anything about the other?" she finally said.

"Yeah. In fact, I was about to ask you about that."

"You haven't even asked me what my first name is," she said, facing him. "How come?"

"I don't know," Griffin said, and he took a big drink of his wine. "Uh, do you like my apartment? I'm having it tastefully done in Early American Legion—"

"Dammit, Griffin, I don't want to make small talk

about your apartment, either." Then she realized the problem. "I don't know what I want." She set the glass of wine down and picked up her purse. "I'm going home."

Surprised, Griffin slowly got to his feet, still holding his glass of wine. Not knowing what else to do and not wanting to look in his eyes, Phoenix stuck out her hand, and they stood there, feeling stupid, shaking hands.

"Aren't you going to say 'Thank you very much and I had a nice time'?" Griffin asked her.

"Good-bye, Griffin," she said, going over to the door, "whoever you are." She walked out into the night, closing the door behind her.

Griffin just stood there, a little dazed. He looked at his glass, started to put it down, then absently started to pick it up again. He suddenly set it down and ran out of his apartment.

Phoenix was just about to get into her car when she saw Griffin run up to her. He abruptly, almost awkwardly, kissed her.

Then he just stood there looking at her a moment.

She looked back and wasn't sure what to think or do. She wasn't sure whether she was mad or happy.

Griffin wordlessly turned and went back into his apartment, and Phoenix got in her car and drove away.

Inside, Griffin heard her driving away. His apartment felt small and stuffy, so he dug in the back of his closet for an old jacket and went out the door again. He walked toward the sea, slowly plodding through the sand, turning the collar of his jacket up against the wind.

He could see by the combined light of condominiums and the moon. Two hundred yards ahead of him on the empty beach, the night tide crashed against the sand.

Phoenix drove along, but not quite as fast as usual. She chewed on her lip, lost in thought. Goddam you, Griffin, she thought to herself, goddam you. She was mad at him for reasons that were not completely his fault.

Phoenix had a blind side, and she knew it. She did her best to be flippant and cynical, because, at heart, she was a complete romantic. And Griffin was getting to her.

It had all started when she was a teen-ager. In her high school, Phoenix was a whiz at math and sciences. But after school, when nobody was watching Sarah the Brain, she would head for the drugstore and stock up on gothic romances. She was a sucker for any paperback where the cover featured a painting of a beautiful, distressed heroine fleeing down a path away from a creepy old house and a full moon.

The older she became, the tougher it was for her. In college, when her sophisticated-acting sorority sisters would go to the movies to laugh at schlocky Hollywood love stories, Phoenix joined them but really felt more like crying.

When it became fashionable to wear jeans and meet a man for a date somewhere, instead of dressing up and having him call on her and all the other old-fashioned bullshit, Phoenix went along with it, acting as modern as anyone else.

But she missed all the old-fashioned bullshit.

The women's movement made things even more complicated for her, especially since Phoenix had always been a believer anyway in strong-minded, independent women who lived their own lives. She wanted to be appreciated for her worth and accomplishments as a person, instead of just her good looks as a woman, and preferred men who viewed her in this way.

It was just that, down deep, she still kind of wanted a knight in shining armor to come clanking along in her direction.

After school, Phoenix traveled a lot, started several different careers, never decided just what to do with herself, and ended up becoming one of the best legal secretaries in New York. But she always had trouble meeting men she could really care about. Her well-thought-out high standards kept getting mixed up with some of her fantasies.

Besides, most businessmen she'd meet were either married or dull or both.

The singles bars weren't any help; the kind of men Phoenix wanted to meet wouldn't be caught dead in a singles bar.

And when girl friends tried to fix her up on blind dates, Phoenix nearly always balked at the idea, without admitting why. Secretly, Phoenix wanted to meet some special man in some really special way. She knew it was silly and sophomoric of her, but that's how she felt.

After several frustrating years, she became tougher on the outside. And even more vulnerable underneath.

Then she met Mike.

He was probably the best-looking, sexiest man she'd ever seen in her life. He was tall, had black hair, green eyes, and a deep, handsome tan that was inexplicably permanent.

He also had an offbeat sense of humor that really appealed to her. But the clincher came when they realized that, just like in the old one-liner, they actually had gone to the same grade school together, twenty years before, hundreds of miles away.

She remembered him. He didn't remember her.

But as if this touch of Fate wasn't enough, after their first date, Mike sent two dozen long-stemmed roses to Phoenix at her office, where all the other women looked at them enviously.

The card said, "This is corny but it usually works."

He was right on both counts.

Mike turned out to be wonderful in bed, and a lot of fun out of bed.

They used to ride the Staten Island ferry a lot, because they both enjoyed it. They went to the zoo, where an interesting thing always happened at the place where they kept the penguins. No matter how many people tried to get the penguins to come near them, they only came close when Mike was around. They always headed straight for him. He and Phoenix always got a kick out of this, but it was the final thing Phoenix needed as some sort of cosmic omen. Obviously, God and half a dozen penguins were trying to tell her something.

She fell totally in love with Mike.

But after many happy months, Mike stopped calling as often as he used to, and Phoenix knew he was seeing other women.

She waited for his calls, almost patiently, seeing him whenever he decided he wanted them to be together, never embarrassing him with her secret faithfulness.

After two years of this, Phoenix met another girl who also had a gigantic crush on Mike. It seems Mike had once sent her roses at the office with a card that said, "This is corny but it usually works." They used to ride the Staten Island ferry, too, because they had both enjoyed it.

But Phoenix loved him, it was too late to change, and she put up with a lot over the next couple of years.

Then one day, whatever Mike's game had been, apparently even he had grown tired of it.

He took Phoenix out to an expensive restaurant and told her he finally felt like getting married. To a pretty, 22-year-old music critic on an underground newspaper. He began to carefully explain how he knew that Phoenix would understand, and how he hoped they would always be friends, and so on. He never got the rest of his speech made. In fact, Phoenix's reaction made him wish he had phoned it in.

Phoenix left New York, mad at herself for acting like a schoolgirl where men were concerned. From now on, she decided, she'd use her head.

She went to Seattle and ended up having a routine doctor's appointment that wasn't exactly routine.

Phoenix now drove through traffic, angry at Griffin, angry at herself, and not too crazy about the world in general. Griffin was sneaking up on her blind side, just when she had decided to be coldly logical where men were concerned.

But there was one thing she was sure about.

Griffin was the kind of guy penguins would love.

Phoenix suddenly made a wild U-turn.

Three other cars screeched to a halt. Tires squealed. Horns honked. Men cursed. But Phoenix ignored them, down-shifted, and headed straight back to the beach.

Griffin, meanwhile, was playing with the sand, sitting on the beach in the dark, near the waves.

He finally spoke, in a soft voice.

"Okay . . . Lord . . . it's been a while, huh?" He stopped, then realized he'd better hurry or he'd get self-conscious and never do it. "Well, it's like this. I've lived thirty-seven years, and so far, I have a few questions . . ."

His voice trailed off. He still felt as though he was probably just talking to himself. No use wondering whether there's really a God or not, he thought to himself, walking on down the beach. He'd know soon enough.

Phoenix knocked loudly on Griffin's door. She waited a minute, then pounded on it.

"Hey, Griffin, c'mon, it's me!"

She tried to peer into a window, but couldn't see. Where the hell could he have gone, she wondered, walking up and down both sides of the street, looking and waiting.

Finally, she went back to his front door, knocked again, then suddenly yelled at the door.

"My first name's Sarah!"

She waited another few moments, looked around again, finally went back to her car, got in, and slowly drove away.

Griffin sat by the edge of the water for over an hour before finally walking back. He made himself some hot chocolate.

The next morning, it took Griffin only a few minutes to pack his car, and he was on the road by nine and heading across the desert toward Albuquerque by noon.

He kept mentally rehearsing what he would say to his wife and kids. Not that topics for conversation would be all that difficult to find when talking to his family, Griffin realized. Once we all chat for a while, he thought, we can always talk about the fact that he'd driven off and left them in the desert many months before, and if there was a real lull in the conversation, they could always kick around the fact that he was dying.

That evening, Griffin parked his car five houses away and just sat in it a while, watching Bobby and Billy shoot baskets. Then he slowly walked toward his home.

He walked across his front yard without saying a word, and one by one, Bobby and Billy stopped playing and stared at their father. The basketball rolled away down the driveway, forgotten, as they rushed into his arms.

Two nights, later, Phoenix returned to Griffin's apartment. It was dark and empty, but she knocked and waited for fifteen minutes before finally leaving. The next night, she waited half an hour.

JULY, 1975—ALBUQUERQUE

Dr. Feinberg's office was the same as it had been the day Griffin got his lab tests, but Dr. Feinberg himself seemed more relaxed as the two men sat and talked.

"How did talking to your family go?"

"Talking to the boys was a lot easier than I thought it would be," Griffin said. "The words were there, somehow, and they seemed to understand. You forget kids have a lot less preconceived fix on how things ought to be. You tell them something that honestly *is,* and they'll nod, and the next things you know, they're showing you something they made at school."

Griffin yawned, then apologized. He and Jean had stayed up most of the night, talking.

"God, that was one weird conversation last night, but it had to be done. Jean and I had to check the details of our taxes and insurance and stuff. We had to decide whether it would be better for her to become a divorcée right away, or wait a while and be a widow."

Griffin and Dr. Feinberg looked at each other.

"You still feel guilty because you're dying, don't you?"

"Yeah."

"You know how little sense that makes, don't you?"

"Yeah."

Dr. Feinberg shrugged, finished stuffing some papers into a big manila envelope, and handed it to Griffin.

"Lab reports, X rays, medical history, and copies of all my notes. Have your Los Angeles doctor contact me any time, of course. Oh, and here are a couple of books you might want to read. One is on cancer itself, the others are terminal case histories, readjustments, and so on."

"Thanks, but I don't know when I can return them." Griffin smiled wryly. "I may never pass this way again."

"Keep the books. You know, there's probably only one other thing that I can do for you," said Dr. Feinberg, getting to his feet.

"What?"

"You like pastrami? There's a terrific place around the corner."

They fought over the check.

JUNE, 1975–LOS ANGELES

The tall doctor walked Phoenix out of his office and down the hospital corridor to her car. She interrupted his detailed report on her latest tests.

"You keep talking to me in terms of blood count," Phoenix said, in a tough way. "Talk to me about time."

They stopped walking. Doctors and nurses swirled around them in the busy hallway.

"You have less than we thought," he said.

Griffin felt better than he had in a long time as he drove out of Albuquerque, but got depressed again by the time he was on the desert highway. The one human characteristic that he'd never realized was so strong was the instinct for making future plans, and he had to keep catching himself.

It was late that night when he parked his car in front of his apartment. He filled his arms with his

71

clothes on hangers, a suitcase, the envelope and books Feinberg had given him, and went over to his apartment door, fumbling around for his keys. Then he noticed the note in the door.

Still awkwardly holding all his junk, he managed one free hand to open the note, angled it toward a nearby street light, and read the scrawled handwriting:

Dwarfs aren't the only ones who get horny. Griffin, where *are* you?

PHOENIX
(since you didn't ask: 555-0759)

Chapter Six

Griffin's face lit up, and with a crazy grin, he fumbled for his keys frantically, nearly dropped his clothes and books, finally found the right key, anxiously tried to get it in the keyhole, had the key upside down, twisted it around, the clothes started slipping, the door finally opened, the clothes and books hit the floor, Griffin hurried in, tripping over them, heading for the phone, turned to pick up his clothes, then left them and went straight for his phone, not bothering to turn on a light, and frantically dialed Phoenix's number.

"Hello?"

"What the hell's your first name, anyway?"

"Griffin!" Phoenix was instantly excited. "What happened to you? I came back, but—"

"It's a long story. I'm home now. Come on over." Griffin reached over and turned on a light.

"Is everything all right?" Phoenix's voice sounded a little strange.

"Sure. Come on over." Griffin waited, listening to the silence on the other end of the phone. "Hey, Phoenix."

"What?"

"This is the best note anyone ever left me."

"Listen, something's come up, and . . . uh . . . I don't think I'd better see you."

"What are you talking about?" Griffin was getting visibly upset. "Come on over. Tell me about it here."

"Look, I don't think I should."

"Come on. We'll talk about it."

"No."

Griffin was tired, hurt, and angry. "Hey, what is it with this on-again, off-again relationship of ours? Phoenix, you're the one who left the note! Now get over here and let's drink wine or make love or something and get on with it!" He stopped for a moment, and thought he heard a muffled sound. "Hey . . . are you crying or something?"

"No, why would I cry?" Phoenix answered in a voice that was obviously trying not to quiver. "I just have a cold, that's all. I shouldn't have left that note."

"Phoenix—"

"Look, I just don't think we should see each other."

Griffin started to say something, but stopped. Again, it went through his mind like a litany: I have no right to ask her to stay. There was a long silence.

"Griffin," she said, at last, "the thing is . . . see . . ." Her voice trailed off.

Griffin waited, feeling strange.

Their relationship, he realized, was like a bizarre game of stud poker, where you see four of the other player's cards, but never the one hidden card until the end. He knew that whatever minor problem in her life was complicating their life, he had her beat, in spades.

"Griffin? Are you still there?" Her voice sounded soft and quiet, like a little girl.

"Yeah, I'm here."

"See . . ." There was another pause. "Never mind. good-bye, Griffin." She hung up.

Griffin slowly put the phone down. It was a while before he picked up his clothes in the doorway.

The next morning, over lumpy oatmeal, Griffin decided flesh-and-blood people were out. Human contact just wouldn't work, not in what he mentally referred to dryly as his particular situation.

He wasn't bitter. It was just that the idea of embracing friends, family, or lovers, taking them into his world, made him feel like a smiling deck steward on the *Titanic*.

He headed for a favorite place where he could get

involved in people's lives without its costing anybody any more than $7.98.

By the time he got to the bookstore, he felt so mellow and detached, the big display of calendars didn't even bother him.

He felt totally removed from the people in twos and threes around him. Griffin had read somewhere that it takes 1/30th of a second for what the human eye perceives to reach the brain, which meant that we're all actually just watching a recording of the past, not the true present as it unfolds. Reality was a movie, badly in need of editing. Suits me fine, Griffin thought, deciding that from now on, he'd just watch.

Griffin loved novels.

To him, they symbolized immortality.

It was illusion, of course, he knew that. Nobody ever really immortalized themselves, not in the long run. Books rot, fall off library shelves, and are swept up by the night janitor. Film gets brittle and cracks; videotape erases. Griffin knew that if you got comfortable and waited long enough, you'd see the "Mona Lisa" thrown in the trash, the Pyramids get flat, and the last copy of *Hamlet* go to help a paper drive. Gibraltar may tumble, the Rockies may crumble, but nobody finds a way to live forever.

But that had been why Griffin had wanted to write a novel and still wished he had one on display in this bookstore.

Griffin had tried to write a novel his very first day at the beach apartment. The title was easy, and he went through the dedication like a buzz saw through hot butter. But starting the first sentence of a novel really threw him.

He studied the classics.

"Call me Ishmael." The first sentence of *Moby Dick* had always impressed Griffin.

He'd stared at his first sheet of blank paper for an hour. Fingers poised above the keys of his typewriter, nervously awaiting inspiration, Griffin finally had realized the best way to begin was just to begin, so he knocked out a quick first sentence and studied it.

"Call me a cab."

That was as far as Griffin got his first day. He went out and tried flying a kite to think about his plot a little more.

His novel-writing class didn't help much. Griffin soon learned from his classmates' attempts that all first novels are either about Unrequited Love, The Military, or A Sensitive Person in a Crass World.

He gave up novels and stocked up on kites instead.

The bookstore, after half an hour of browsing, was a big disappointment. Every title was cleverly tied in with either Zen, needlepoint, or the C.I.A. Griffin bought two paperbacks, a thick classic he'd always meant to read, and a thin police thriller.

He grabbed a hamburger and a newspaper and headed back to his apartment, where he carefully planned the rest of the day. Read until 5:30, then go to a movie, taking advantage of the early-bird prices, then rush home in time to watch an old Humphrey Bogart movie on TV. Secure that every minute of his day ensured both entertainment and isolation, Griffin opened *War and Peace* and decided that the rest of the book had better be a little snappier than the opening sentence.

The second Phoenix stepped inside The Sunset Home for the Retired, she was sorry she had come.

The place smelled like old cheese.

Several middle-aged people were awkwardly saying good-bye to someone wrapped in a blanket in a wheelchair. The ancient, white-haired person was so old Phoenix could not tell whether it was a man or a woman. She knew the departing relatives probably felt guilty about putting Grandma/Grampa in a home, but knew they'd hate to have him/her in their own lives every day.

The wonderful thing about dying young and childless, Phoenix thought while looking for the main office, is that you don't have to worry about being a burden to your children in your old age.

A stern, matronly woman told Phoenix how nice it was for her to volunteer to help with the elderly, reading to them, writing letters for them, or just talking with them. Some had not had any real visitors of their own in years.

Phoenix's first assignment was to read an article from *Reader's Digest* to nice old Mr. Quimberly in Room 206. Nice old Mr. Quimberly in Room 206 just sat up in bed, not at all responsive, so Phoenix began reading "I Am Joe's Urinary Tract," reminding herself of her decision that morning.

The phone call from Griffin had just happened, causing her to have a terrible night. She had stayed awake, conscious of the empty space between herself and the four walls of her apartment. When dawn finally came, she had realized the importance of people to her, now more than ever.

She decided to almost blindly throw herself into helping people, getting involved, unselfishly using her time trying to do her small part to make the world a little better place in which to die.

Phoenix had called several charity organizations, assuming it would take them a few days to find her something, but an hour and a half later, she found herself walking into the nursing home.

Phoenix looked up from her *Reader's Digest* article and noticed that nice old Mr. Quimberly's head was slumped forward on his chest and that his nice old eyes were closed.

Phoenix ran for a nurse in panic.

The nurse explained that he had just fallen asleep; that was why they read to him.

Phoenix then spent the longest hour of her life listening to one old woman say how much she wished she could get a new cat. She wanted it to replace her old cat, Cinnamon (a Persian), she got to replace Rosemary (a tabby), which had once been a replacement for Parsley (a calico), which she had gotten as a replacement for her daughter (an ingrate), who had grown up and left.

Next, in the sitting room, Phoenix was introduced to Mr. Maloney, a man of eighty-seven. He sat there with a certain sad dignity. Phoenix asked him if he wanted to watch TV or talk or anything. He was uninterested, never saying much. She tried chatting about his family, but a nurse came up and said, "Here you are, Mr. Maloney, time for your pill." He took it and answered Phoenix's questions about his friends and family. The conversation was a mistake; they were all dead. Phoenix and he just sat there for a moment, then he slowly turned to her and simply said, "There is no one left to call me Robert."

Phoenix was then assigned to talk with a man who drooled a lot, then a woman who wanted help writing a letter. Phoenix got a pad and pen ready, smiling, waiting, but as the letter began, it was obvious she had no one to write to. The old woman then picked out an ad in the back of a magazine and asked Phoenix to help her write to it. She said she loved getting mail. Phoenix quickly helped her ask for a free pamphlet where she could learn meat-cutting in her own home in her spare time.

Phoenix then told the head nurse she was going to lunch for a few minutes, knowing she'd never come back.

She headed straight for the door, pausing only to throw a big smile and a wave to Mr. Maloney in the next room, yelling, "So long, Bob! Keep your ass out of trouble!"

Mr. Maloney looked up at her and slowly waved, smiling for the first time in years.

Driving away, Phoenix realized how hard she was to please; she didn't want to grow old and didn't want to die young.

Driving along felt good, but Phoenix realized she was right back where she had started from, except she was now conscious of a strange, anxious feeling.

She drove past a grade school, watching kids playing at recess, and smiled, remembering a similar feeling once when she was a little girl.

Her entire class, somehow, had begun playing a game they had invented which they called "Battlefield." It had become the rage of the entire third grade, played on a huge, open field by the school. Some undefined war was going on on the field, but back by the school wall, where they all waited, it was safe. One by one, the boys, brave Soldiers every one, would run across the field, get shot, and fall valiantly, with no small amount of dust-raising. They had to lie still until one of the girls, as a Nurse, would run out, touch her favorite boy, thus saving his life, and the two would run back together to safety. Phoenix recognized it now as being the only acceptable way for a girl to show how much she liked a particular boy.

One afternoon, after the game had just begun, Phoenix (then a small little girl named Sarah who wished she had pigtails) had a profound idea. Suppose a Nurse got shot? In real wars, nurses must get shot, too. Then she could lie there and see if Jack Horstmeyer or maybe even Mike Cunningham would come out, touch her, and save her life. She waited until Marci MacDonald, the prettiest girl in the school, had finished her turn as Nurse, then ran at top speed across the field, ignoring the fallen bodies of the warriors around her. She suddenly yelled, clasped what would someday become her bosom, flew through the air, tumbled head-over-heels, and when the dust settled, she lay still, having just made the greatest fall ever seen. The other kids just stopped and stared; Nurses don't get shot. But there she lay. The game continued, as usual. Phoenix lay there, unmoving, untouched, humiliated for the next forty-five minutes. It doesn't have to be Mike Cunningham; Jack Horstmeyer would be fine, she thought. Toward the end of the recess, red-faced, but not having moved an inch on her own, she'd have settled for Billy Hetzler, even. But nobody came.

Phoenix smiled at the memory, wryly amused at why that feeling seemed vaguely familiar now, and decided to stop for lunch. Instinctively, she started to order her usual ground sirloin and cottage cheese. She suddenly ordered a banana split instead. What the hell.

Phoenix headed for a supermarket next. Normally, Phoenix ate most of her meals out, where she could use her credit cards, hating to cook for just one person. But tonight she figured she'd spoil herself a little, and she enjoyed wheeling her shopping cart around, buying only her favorite foods.

That was fun for a while, but then she came to the

meat section. Phoenix was about to reach for one filet mignon, then noticed the woman select four. On her other side, a young woman was comparing several, and finally decided on three good ones.

Phoenix put a second steak in her shopping cart.

Griffin had abandoned *War and Peace* on page three and was now nearly finished with the police thriller. He drained his third can of beer for the afternoon, crushed it with one hand, then lobbed it up toward the little basketball goal above the wastebasket. And missed.

There was a knock at the door.

Griffin, slouched in his chair, did not move.

"Who is it?" he yelled.

"Sarah."

"Who?"

"Sarah."

Griffin sat there, puzzled.

"Sarah who?"

"Sarah Phoenix."

Griffin, happily surprised, began to get up, but then stopped himself.

"I thought we were off-again," he said, smiling, but trying to sound serious.

"Well, we're on-again," Phoenix said, from outside, impatiently. "Open the door, dammit."

Griffin opened the door, and Phoenix marched right in, hardly looking at him, and headed for the kitchen, carrying two big grocery bags.

"What's that?"

"Dinner," she said.

Chapter Seven

The sun had been down for about forty minutes, long enough to turn on a light and do the dishes, but Griffin and Phoenix hadn't bothered with either. It was moody and quiet in Griffin's apartment, and they just sat on the floor, enjoying the wine and the twilight. Griffin was sprawled on his back, his wineglass balanced on his stomach. Phoenix was leaning against a chair, playing with some kite string.

". . . anyway, at least I managed not to do the cliché of falling in love with my boss," Phoenix said. "But I did fall in love with a lawyer who had his office just down the hall. He had his own practice and I'd have to walk past his door every day. 'Cunningham & Totten, Attorneys-at-Law' it said on the frosted glass. Frosted glass . . ." she mused. "Very fitting . . . anyway, that cost me five years of my life, waiting around for him."

Phoenix was quiet for a while. Griffin didn't say anything. He just poured each of them a little more wine. It wasn't dark yet, just dusky. They weren't drunk yet, just mellow.

"Anyway," Phoenix finally said, "the son of a bitch even dumped me the way they advise in men's magazines. You know, in a classy restaurant so there won't be a scene?" Phoenix smiled to herself. "When I got finished, there were little pieces of scene sticking to the walls and ceiling . . ." She laughed.

"So you came to L.A.?" Griffin asked.

81

"No, for some stupid reason, I went to Seattle. I thought New York was dirty and Seattle sounded clean. I was confusing clean with wet. Things didn't . . . go well up there, so I came here." Phoenix took a sip of her wine, then mumbled, almost to herself. "Jesus . . . that was the story of my life, and it wasn't very interesting."

It was quiet for a few minutes. Griffin looked at the nearby dishes, seeing the remains of two steaks and some twice-baked potatoes. He considered taking them into the other room, then reconsidered; brave decisions are made in this world when the only alternative is washing dishes.

"I've got a wife and two kids in Albuquerque," Griffin suddenly said. "We've been separated for a while."

Phoenix didn't react one way or the other.

"Is that where you went?" she asked.

"Yeah."

"So, how are . . . things?"

Griffin sighed.

"My wife and I had quite a scene. Then I had to tell my two boys something I should have told them a long time ago."

"The facts of life?" Phoenix said, teasing.

"Yeah," Griffin said, wryly. "One of them."

They didn't say anything for a few moments.

"I can't figure out what you're doing, Griffin. You just lie around here."

"Well, you don't work for a living, either. I got a brother that's a soft touch. What's your excuse?"

"I've still got a little money saved," she said. It was her personal nest egg. She had planned to surprise her new husband with it in New York. Sometimes life isn't full of surprises. "I've got a lot of credit cards that I mainly live off of. Unless I overdo it, it can take almost a year for a credit card company to finally nail you."

"But what happens in a year or so?"

"Oh, I'll worry about that then," she said, trying to make it light, trying to think of a fast way to change the subject. "Hey, let's go do something . . ."

Griffin just looked at her, not understanding.

"You know," she said, getting irritated for having to spell it out for him, "like a date?"

"A *date*?"

It took a while for Griffin to catch on, but once he got the hang of it, they headed for a movie. This time, he said, they'd pay for their tickets and go in the front way, just to be different.

There was a long line to buy the tickets.

"Can we sit in the back row of the balcony and neck?" Phoenix asked him.

"No."

"Why not?"

"Because this is only our first date," Griffin said, buying the tickets, "and you might lose respect for me."

They really didn't care about sitting in the balcony, until they saw a small purple rope strung across the stairs and a sign that said, "Balcony Closed."

They had the whole balcony to themselves, of course.

But instead of sitting in the back row and necking, they sat in the first row and carefully dropped Milk Duds on people's heads.

An hour later, they were tearing around a go-cart track at thirty miles per hour, six inches off the ground, the wind in their hair, fire in their eyes, bugs in their teeth.

The race was on: it wasn't how you played the game, it was who won, and they both knew it.

Phoenix took the curves at speeds that several of Newton's Laws of Motion frowned upon, and Griffin was right behind her, eating her dust, not liking it. He had selected his go-cart because it had a slightly bigger engine and better gear ratio. Phoenix had chosen hers because green was her favorite color.

Phoenix had won all six laps because she had the faster car.

Griffin floored it coming off of one curve of the figure-eight-shaped track, trying to get in position to pass her on the straightaway. He was almost even with her as they went screaming into the next curve, but

Griffin let up on the gas a little, something Phoenix never did.

The guy that owned the place, known as Maxey the Tattoo, yawned. He decided to give the two of them one more lap. They were the only people on the course. It was late, and he'd been about to close up when Griffin had talked him into letting them take a few laps. Maxey the Tattoo's partner would be arriving soon with an old go-cart they used for parts, and they had several hours' worth of work ahead of them yet. Still, it was fun to watch two adults having this much fun, hunched over the tiny cars.

Usually, the place just got junior-high kids. Maxey the Tattoo spent his whole life running different amusement rides for children. He hated kids.

He flashed the light on and off twice, signaling Griffin and Phoenix their time was up and to pull in.

They ignored him.

He flashed the lights again, waving.

They raced on. Griffin was about to catch her, also having learned to floor it on the curves. They were neck and neck and not about to quit now.

Irritated, Maxey the Tattoo stepped out on the track, under one of the lights, and started to wave Phoenix down.

You can scale the north face of the Matterhorn in winter; you can have a mechanic tell you the 69¢ part was simple to install so there's no charge for labor; you can regain your innocence. But you can't just stroll out on a go-cart track and wave Phoenix down; Maxey the Tattoo dived to one side at the last second into some bales of hay and a stack of tires, realizing that he had nearly made a statistic of himself.

He was trying to decide whether to punch the guy out when they ran out of gas, slug the broad, or call the police, when his partner arrived in a pickup truck at the far end of the track. The partner unfastened the gateway, moved some bales of hay aside, and started to drive the truck in to unload the old go-cart in back.

Phoenix ran for daylight; she was through the fence and tearing across the sidewalks and racing down the street. Griffin was right behind her.

Maxey the Tattoo and his partner just stared, dumb-founded, as Griffin and Phoenix continued their race into the night.

Griffin won.

Griffin sat on the edge of the bed naked. Phoenix lay beside him, holding a sheet over her nude body. She leaned up on one elbow and gently put her hand on his back.

"Hey . . ." she said, softly. "It's all right." Griffin almost flinched at the touch, but didn't look at her.

"What else can you say?" he said.

"I mean, really. Don't worry about it, okay?"

"You gotta say it's all right," Griffin said, irritated. "There's no other way you can act. That's probably the advice in all the *women's* magazines."

It was quiet for a moment as Phoenix took her hand away. Then Griffin turned and looked at her, touching her thigh.

"Hey, I'm sorry. I shouldn't take it out on you. It's just that . . . well, something happened a few months ago, and I've had trouble ever since . . ."

"Hey," Phoenix said, in the warmest voice Griffin had ever heard a woman use. "Holding is nice."

They smiled. He got back under the sheet and put his arm around her shoulders and she snuggled close. Somewhat content, they fell asleep.

They wore makeshift robes while eating breakfast. Griffin was wrapped up in his favorite old comfortable jacket. Phoenix wore an old quilt off Griffin's bed, and socks. She was in the middle of some story.

"I mean, how would you like to be halfway through a bowl and glance down and notice little tiny bugs crawling around? The cereal box was full of them."

"Were they good?"

"Actually," Phoenix said, "the real problem with eating insects and cereal is that once you've eaten all the bugs, well, then you're left with, you know, cereal . . ."

They went back to digging around inside their cantaloupes. There was a silence, except for some minor slurping.

The mood changed a little, and Phoenix finally spoke.

"Hey."

"What?"

"What's something you've always wanted to do? I mean like when you were fourteen and didn't know any better?"

"Seriously?"

"Yeah."

Griffin seriously shoved his spoon into his cantaloupe rind, seriously put it aside, and then finally answered seriously.

"Well, when I was fourteen, I used to daydream in chemistry class about being invisible and sneaking down to the girls' locker room."

"Griffiin."

He thought for a moment.

"The other thing I used to want to do—and I haven't thought about this in years—was to hop a freight train, just to see where it took me."

Phoenix leaned closer, with a strange smile on her face.

"So what's stopping us?"

Griffin just stared at her.

It was a beautiful day—blue sky, white clouds, the works.

Railroad tracks curved around a hill in that part of town where you're almost out of the city but not yet in the country. Griffin and Phoenix ran down the tracks toward a small hill.

"We're sure going to feel silly if a train doesn't come along," Phoenix said, already panting a little.

"We'll feel worse if it does."

Griffin wore an old sweatshirt and jeans and ran ahead, continually glancing over his shoulder down the track.

"We haven't missed it, have we? I mean, I didn't make us late, did I?"

"The station said there was a 3:40. What took you so long, anyway?"

"Well, I couldn't figure out what to wear."

"You're kidding."

"I changed clothes three times," Phoenix said. "I've never hopped a freight before."

She had finally selected something in your basic gold football jersey, blue jeans, sneakers that are really quite chic, a blue-and-red plaid scarf, and a bag (full of sandwiches and a small Thermos of coffee) smartly styled in khaki with an over-the-shoulder strap.

"You look fine," Griffin said. "If we live through this, we'll get arrested, anyway."

"Sure wish you wouldn't try to whitewash everything, just to keep my spirits up . . ." she mumbled to herself.

Then Griffin stopped, holding up his hand.

"Hey . . ." He was listening. Phoenix caught up to him and stood there listening, too. At first, all she could hear was just the wind and a few birds.

Then she heard it, too, faintly in the distance, gradually getting louder.

Griffin's train.

They both slowly turned and looked at each other, getting excited.

"Now what do we do?" she finally said.

"I don't know, but it's time to do something."

He steered her over to some bushes. They ducked out of sight, then peered back down the track. They were both nervous and happy.

"Where do you suppose it's going?" she said quietly.

"Now you're getting it," Griffin said, moving out away from the bushes a little. The sound of the train grew louder. They could even hear the whistle on Griffin's train go off twice, but couldn't see it quite yet.

Then, around the curve . . .

The engine was black and yellow, the headlight was on, and it looked more like a cyclops than a train as it came tearing down the track toward them.

Scared, excited, they stepped back into the bushes, as though the engineer could see them and read their minds.

87

The train screamed past them.

It was immense, a giant rushing wall of steel and iron, only ten feet away. The sound filled their skulls and the wheels went grinding by, a monster gnashing its teeth.

"Looks pretty big!" Phoenix yelled to Griffin.

"We don't have to stop it," he yelled back, even though they were standing only a foot apart, "we just have to jump on the side of it."

The train seemed like it would never end, rushing by forever. Griffin couldn't see any way to jump on the smooth-sided oil tankers. He looked down the track. Coming their way were the traditional freight cars, complete with handrails up the side.

If a person could run fast enough, time it just right, grab a handrail that wouldn't break off, have strong enough hands, jump on just right, catch a bottom rung quickly with your feet, and stay out of the wheels, it was a cakewalk.

Griffin nudged Phoenix, then started running along after a freight car, just after a flatcar flew past them. Phoenix took a deep breath and started running after him.

Griffin ran dangerously close to the freight car, the handles and ladder rungs within touching distance. He tried to spot a solid foothold, too. He could think of better ways to spend an afternoon than being dragged to death.

Griffin ran as fast as he could but was running out of breath and running out of train.

He stuck his hand out toward an iron bar on the ladder, put on one last burst of speed which he didn't have in him, got a tight grip on it, then committed his weight to it, making the jump.

His grip started to slip, and he scrambled with his other hand for the ladder rung, his feet flailing in the wind.

Then his right foot caught a bottom rung inches from the whirling steel wheels, and he pulled himself completely on, hanging on tight for a second, feeling very alive.

He swung around and climbed up the ladder. After

two rungs, he got cocky and quickly climbed to the very top of the boxcar, peering over the edge, the wind in his hair, a proud, happy smile on his face.

He watched the world go by, happy as a kid with his first train set.

Then he looked back down the track and saw Phoenix.

She was exhausted, running as fast as she could, but falling back.

He quickly climbed back down the ladder, hooked his right arm into the ladder rung, then extended his left hand out toward Phoenix, who was forty feet back.

She saw his hand, stretched out to help her, and she tried running faster, narrowing the distance between them to thirty feet, then twenty.

She was reaching out her hand, too.

But the speeding train was relentlessly charging on, not giving away any points for sincerity. You either made it or you didn't.

Phoenix was being left behind.

She waved for him to go on, without her. She lapsed into a half-walk, half-trot, completely spent.

Griffin watched her shrink in the distance, put his face to the wind, savoring the moment one last time, looked at the blurred landscape he was flying past, and jumped.

Chapter Eight

Griffin sailed into space, hit the ground, tumbled over and over and finally made a beautiful three-point landing (right ankle, left arm, rear end) against an embankment, then slowly slid down the grassy incline on his back, more than a little stunned.

Ignoring a pain in his ankle, Griffin looked up, exhausted, dazed as his train went roaring on past. It filled the sky; the sunlight flashed between the freight cars across his face.

He smiled proudly.

His train was going by.

As it disappeared down the track, Griffin noticed that he was near an old junkyard full of a million rusty cars. Never even got out of the city, Griffin thought, but, Jesus, that was fun.

He lay there, panting, knowing he'd be sore in the morning, knowing he wouldn't mind a bit. He turned and saw the panting figure of Phoenix slowly running toward him. He tried to get up, but then decided just to lie there in the grass and the sunlight; the nice thing about hopping a freight is that it feels so good when it's over.

A few moments later, Phoenix slowly staggered over within ten feet of him and collapsed in the grass. They were panting as they half-crawled toward each other.

"I'm sorry, Griffin," Phoenix said, trying to catch her breath. "I'm sorry . . ."

Griffin just grinned at her, happily.

"I'm really sorry," she went on, "I wanted you to make your train . . ."

Griffin pulled her closer.

"Hey . . . I made it."

So you did, she thought, smiling. He kissed her and she kissed back.

Then they heard the sound of an old man cackling.

They looked up toward the junkyard and saw an old hobo. He was pointing at them, slapping his knee, and laughing to himself.

Griffin and Phoenix stared.

He wore a strange hat, torn clothes, and carried a mysterious bulging sack. He stood near his makeshift lean-to made from rusty car fenders. At his side was a three-legged dog.

Griffin and Phoenix exchanged looks, then got to their feet. Griffin suddenly winced and almost fell, yelling "Oww!"

This sent the old hobo into new fits of laughter.

"What's the matter?" Phoenix asked, as Griffin leaned on her.

"My ankle. I must have sprained it or . . ." Griffin suddenly turned to the hobo. "What the hell are you laughing at?"

"*You,* ya damn fool! You try to hop the 3:40 to nowhere on the wrong side of the hill and you fall on your ass doing it! Then you start smoochin'!" The hobo cackled some more.

"Can you walk?" Phoenix asked.

"No, but I got a terrific limp," Griffin said to her, putting his arm around her for support. They awkwardly tried to limp away, but the old hobo stopped laughing and hurried toward them, digging around in his strange sack.

"Hey, don't run off! Not with a bum ankle! I can help . . . maybe . . ."

The old hobo began pulling things from his sack, mumbling to himself as he produced a yo-yo, a broken pencil sharpener, a plumber's friend, a hubcap, a large natural sponge, a ball-peen hammer . . .

"Think I got me a danged ol' Ace bandage," he mumbled as he dug around. "I kin wrap it for ya.

92

Used to be an ambulance driver. Back in the first war in Italy. I was sixteen. I knew Ernie Hemingway, you know, the writer? He was just another snot-nosed kid like me—"

"Thanks," Phoenix said, "but I think—"

"Here it is!" The old hobo suddenly produced an Ace ankle bandage and, miracle of miracles, it even looked clean. "Take off your shoe, young fella."

Griffin shrugged, carefully sat down in the grass and took off his shoe. The old hobo expertly began to wrap the bandage. "Yeah, just looks sprained," he said. "Never rid them rails afore, have ya?"

"No. First time."

"I've been a bo' ridin' the rails over forty years," the old hobo said, proudly. "Had a son once. He was a hobo like me. Then he settled and had a son that growed to be a goddammed worthless hippie. There. That should do it."

"Thank you very much," Griffin said, checking the bandage. It was wrapped good and tight.

"I think we can make it back to the car now," Phoenix said.

"Car!" The old hobo stared in amazement. "You got a car and you jump the 3:40 to nowhere?"

"Just thought we'd try it," Griffin said, almost apologetically.

"Just thought you'd try it . . ." The old hobo repeated the words, shaking his head to himself. "Now I know it's all gone . . . it's all over, for sure."

As the old hobo stared off into the distance, Phoenix helped Griffin to his feet.

"Let's see if you can walk."

Griffin managed to hobble a little, experimenting with how much weight he could hold, as the old hobo began to mumble to himself.

"Ol' Ernie musta knowed it was all over for him, too . . . sucked on a shotgun one mornin' up in Idaho . . . never been there, hear it's pretty country . . . suicide, that's what it were with Ernie, suicide . . ."

Suddenly uncomfortable, Griffin and Phoenix turned to leave. "Well, thanks again," Griffin said.

"Glad I could help," the old hobo said. "How about givin' me five dollars for my trouble?"

"What?"

"Parts, labor, my medical training . . . five bucks is dirt cheap and you damn well know it."

Griffin and Phoenix looked at each other, then Phoenix dug in her pocket and stuffed a bill in the old hobo's hand.

"Here's a dollar," she said. "It'll have to do."

"It will . . ." said the old hobo. "Weekend hobos . . . I don't believe it . . . you know, I called ol' Ernie once after he got famous and all . . ." He paused, then added sadly, "He didn't remember me . . ."

"We will," Phoenix said. "Thanks."

They turned and slowly headed back toward Griffin's car. The old hobo watched them go, then suddenly started yelling after them.

"Ain't got me a shotgun . . . I keep thinkin' one night I'll get sense enough to lay my sleepin' board across them tracks and catch forty winks . . . might just take my snooze in front of the 3:40 to nowhere!" His tone got strangely hostile and louder, the more he spoke. "Ain't that where you was headed? Mebbe I'll see you there! You'll be there! You'll see! You and your goddam dollar bills!"

Griffin and Phoenix never looked back at the disturbing specter of the old hobo, waving his fist at them.

Phoenix drove, so Griffin wouldn't have to use his ankle.

"You want to get it X-rayed?" Phoenix asked as they drove home.

"I'm sure it's just sprained. That crazy old bastard wrapped it good, though."

"You think he really knew Ernest Hemingway?"

"Nah," Griffin said. "He was probably thinking of someone else. Jack London, Gore Vidal, somebody." Griffin paused. "You ever thought about suicide?"

"Yes," said Phoenix, without hesitating.

"Oh." There was a sudden change in the mood that made Griffin very uncomfortable. Goddam that old fool. "Hey, let's order a pizza tonight, okay?"

"Yeah," Phoenix said, not looking at him. "Hey,

listen . . ." Griffin watched her, knowing something was wrong. She was driving under the speed limit.

"I don't know if we should be seeing so much of each other," she finally said.

"We're having one of our strange conversations again, Phoenix. In the last thirty seconds, we've gone from pizza to suicide to I-hope-we'll-always-be-friends—"

"I'm serious, Griffin."

They just drove along, not saying anything.

"Are you sure?" Griffin said, wondering if it might be the best thing for both of them. It began inside his head: I have no right to . . .

"I'm not sure of anything," she finally said.

"We'll talk about it."

The hot shower felt good so Griffin took his time washing his hair. He stood there, letting it pour over him, slowly washing, turning his face up into the water. Then he stuck his head out of the water and yelled into the next room.

"Pizza here yet?"

He thought he heard the answer but wasn't sure. He shifted his weight carefully, sticking his head out again, careful of his ankle. "What?"

"I said no!" Phoenix yelled from the next room.

Griffin stuck his head back in the shower, then back out again. "You're awfully quiet. Anything wrong?"

"No," hollered Phoenix from Griffin's living room. She was still dressed in her freight-hopping clothes and was wandering around, bored.

No, nothing's wrong, she thought to herself, except I'm too weak to run any more so it's getting closer, which scares the hell out of me, that's all. Otherwise, everything's just peachy keen.

Phoenix wandered over to Griffin's makeshift bookshelf, where he was in the habit of leaving his keys and change and stuff. She picked up his key chain—a round, laminated green clover leaf—and idly held it up to the light.

"How come you always carry around this three-leaf clover?" she yelled toward the shower.

"I've had it for years . . ." Griffin yelled back.

Phoenix put it down, bored with it, and began looking through Griffin's paperbacks, but Griffin wasn't finished talking about it.

"I first got it a long time ago to kid my brother," Griffin yelled, chattering away from the shower. "George started to carry around a dumb rabbit's foot . . ."

Then Phoenix noticed something in the corner of the little bookshelf. Several hardback books were hidden behind the paperbacks in the far corner. She took them out and looked at them, while Griffin droned on in the next room.

"I used to tease him a lot," Griffin continued from the shower, obliviously splashing his way down memory lane. "I warned him once that it's bad luck to walk under a black cat and, to this day, he never has . . ."

Phoenix didn't hear anything.

Numb, she read the titles of Griffin's hidden books: *Approaching Death: Twenty-Six Case Histories*. The next book was titled: *Attitudes Toward Terminal Illnesses*. And with fingers that began to shake a little, Phoenix turned the last book around and read the title: *When the End Is Near*.

Her expression slowly went from stunned and puzzled to angry. She suddenly whirled around and headed for the bathroom door.

Griffin was still happily soaping away in a fool's paradise when Phoenix kicked in the bathroom door, startling him.

She was in a total and complete rage: hurt, angry, humiliated, furious, tears in her eyes, screaming at the top of her lungs.

"Goddam you! How the hell did you find out? Who gave you the right to snoop around in my life?"

Griffin was utterly confused. "What are you talking about—"

Phoenix began hitting and kicking at him through the opaque shower curtain, screaming louder and louder.

"Why did you do it? I loved you, you sneaky bastard, and you're playing some sick game!" Griffin was unsuccessfully trying to dodge the hitting and kicking, his protests never heard. "Next time you pull this, hide your damn books better!"

She ripped the shower curtain away, hurled the heavy books at him, and stormed out of the bathroom.

The books clobbered Griffin one by one, then fell to the wet shower floor. Griffin lowered his arms, looking completely astounded. He picked up a soggy book and almost visibly turned white. He recognized the other books at his feet, half-floating in the soapy water.

Then the front door slammed.

Griffin, confused about what had just happened, was instantly sure of one thing: Phoenix had just headed out the front door and this time she wasn't coming back.

He rushed out of the shower, leaving it on, and grabbed a pair of pants on a hook. He ran through the living room, putting on his pants, grabbing his old jacket as he went by, wincing from the pain in his sprained ankle.

He hurried into the night, his hair and body still covered with soapy wet water, and looked around wildly.

No Phoenix.

Shivering in the night air and trying to ignore his swollen ankle, Griffin painfully limped up the street, peering into the darkness.

"Phoenix! Phoenix!" he yelled "Where are you?"

He quickly limped back in the other direction, toward the beach, frantically looking around.

"Phoenix!"

No answer. He couldn't find her.

"PHOENIX!"

Nothing. She was gone.

Then, out of the corner of his eye, he saw a figure out on the sand, heading out across the beach. Ignoring his ankle, he hurried after the figure, hoping it was she.

Phoenix marched across the sand, heading straight away from Griffin, ignoring his yelling behind her. Angrily, she rubbed the moisture from the edge of her eyes.

Fifty feet behind her, Griffin began limping after her.

"Phoenix!" he yelled. "Will you wait a minute?"

She didn't answer or look back. She just kept walking as fast as she could through the sand.

"Phoenix, *please!*"

"Go to hell, Griffin!"

"What happened? What—"

"Go hang around another death class, you creep!" she screamed over her shoulder.

"I don't know what—"

"Get yourself some other loser!"

Griffin tried to hurry, but couldn't trudge through the sand without feeling his purple ankle with every step.

"Phoenix! Wait!" There was desperation in his voice. He couldn't keep up with her. "I don't know what you're doing!"

Phoenix just continued marching across the beach, but yelled back over her shoulder, angry and embarrassed. "You know I'm dying you . . . you . . ." Her voice started to crack. "Leave me alone!"

Truly confused, Griffin stopped and stared.

"Sarah! You aren't the one who's dying! *I* am!"

He started after her, moving fast, forgetting the pain.

Physically weak and confused by what Griffin had just yelled, Phoenix still tried to get away from Griffin and the strange sense of shame she felt about her own death.

Forty feet behind her, Griffin moved as fast as he could, gaining on her.

Both were exhausted, but Griffin finally tackled her and they both pitched forward in the sand. Phoenix tried to whirl away, more furious than ever, pounding at him. He tried to grab her hands.

"Goddam you!" she screamed.

She flailed away at him, blindly.

"Phoenix, stop it!"

She finally stopped struggling as he got a hold on her arms, pinning her down.

Griffin yelled into her face.

"We're not going to move until you tell me what the hell is going on!"

Angry, Phoenix tried to twist away, but Griffin held

her down. She got a leg free and kicked him in his sprained ankle, wrenching an arm free, but Griffin grabbed her again. She finally realized she wasn't going anyplace. She glared at him, and he glared right back, and there was a long silence. Finally, Phoenix screamed at him.

"How can you act like you don't know!"

"Don't know *what*!"

"That I've got leukemia! What the hell else are those books for if you don't know!"

Griffin looked at her, stunned. "Leukemia . . ." He let go her arms and leaned off to one side of her. There was something very believable about his amazed tone of voice and his stunned expression, which confused Phoenix even more.

"Goddammit, Griffin, if you didn't know, how come you've got those books and how come you've been so nice to me!"

Quietly, still dazed, Griffin gave the only answer he could, speaking very softly and very slowly.

"I don't know whether to laugh or cry . . . Phoenix, those books are for me because my chest is full of cancer, and I haven't been nice to you. I love you."

It was Phoenix's turn to have a stunned expression, her anger turning to a sad kind of confusion.

"*That's* why I was at that class," Griffin said. "But I never thought that *you* . . ."

He let it trail off as they looked at each other with an expression much more painful than the mistrust and disbelief of a few seconds before: belief.

Phoenix hesitantly reached out for Griffin, gently touching him, as though he might break. Griffin watched her trembling hand touching him, gently. He suddenly grabbed her, pulling her very close to him and she held on tight, very tight, and they lay still, hanging on for dear life.

"Oh God," she heard herself saying, "what are we going to do . . ."

Griffin answered softly. "I guess we're going to die."

They lay there in the sand and the darkness for a long time.

Chapter Nine

Finally, they headed back to the apartment. It was all too much; they said nothing.

Griffin washed and dried himself off, and Phoenix just sat in the overstuffed chair, staring at the glass-blown winged horse on the shelf, watching its strange dark shadow from a nearby street light. She was still staring at it twenty minutes later when the pizza arrived.

They ate in silence, each sitting in a far corner of Griffin's living room, watching each other.

That night, they just lay in bed. Griffin stared at the ceiling. Phoenix lay on her side, staring at the wall.

When Phoenix woke up the next morning, it was nearly noon. She saw Griffin out on the beach, trying to fly his kite. She slowly got dressed and made some coffee.

She sat staring at her coffee and became very conscious of her extreme apathy. Nothing mattered. Nothing. What she felt transcended indifference and took her to some new chilly, foggy place that frightened her.

She wanted her mother.

Phoenix loved her mother, but she didn't like her. Mrs. Walter Phoenix was a terrific wife and a lousy mother. Ignoring honest instincts, she had raised her daughter by the book, always responding to her child the way A Mother Should. During some undergraduate argument, Phoenix had once accused her of being a machine that made mother noises. Phoenix had instantly apologized, feeling really bad about striking someone on and about the head and shoulders with so much truth at one time.

Three cigarettes into the phone call, Phoenix knew she'd made a mistake.

"Mother, stop saying he wasn't good enough for me. This is long distance and you've said that four times."

Phoenix invariably chain-smoked while talking to her mother. She had once considered chain-drinking.

"Anyway, Mother, that's all over. Look, I've got some news . . . I wasn't going to tell you but, well, recently—What? . . . No, it's disconnected because I'm not living there any more. It's a long story, but it's part of what I want to—What? All right, Mother. I'm staying with a man I care very much about, and . . . Mother . . . *Mother* . . ."

Phoenix listened to the automatic mother noises, feeling hurt and getting angry. "For God's sake, I'm thirty-four years old . . . Mother . . ."

Phoenix quietly hung up, and the phone made a soft click. She'd decided years ago that as long as you didn't make a loud slam, you weren't really hanging up on someone.

Phoenix wandered around the apartment, feeling more hollow than ever.

She started to brush her hair, then set the brush back down. She didn't care that much about how she looked. Phoenix looked out of the window at Griffin, thinking for the thousandth time since last night: *he* is going to die.

Griffin, two hundred yards away, was awkwardly churning up the sand, trying to get one of his stupid kites in the air. But the kite wasn't gaining any altitude, no matter how hard Griffin tried.

Phoenix turned away from the window listlessly, not watching Griffin any more.

Griffin was jerking on the kite string a few seconds later, when suddenly his stride faltered.

Nothing is more frightening in this world than a pain you've never felt before coming from inside your chest.

Griffin stopped running, mouth open, gasping, afraid.

He slowly reached up, reaching for his chest, as though he could grab the pain and stop it.

Inside, Phoenix looked around the room again, looked at her watch, then smiled at herself for the unconscious gesture. She took off her watch and put it on an empty top shelf of a cupboard and left it there, then turned and glanced back out at Griffin.

From this distance, all she could see was that Griffin was just standing there, his back to her, letting the kite swirl down toward the water.

Griffin, dammit, the kite . . . she thought to herself, don't just stand there and watch it, come on, try!

Swooping and falling in jerky motions, the kite was about twenty or thirty feet above the water. Then fifteen.

"Come on, Griffin," Phoenix said out loud. "Don't you quit on me . . ."

Phoenix ran to the door, threw it open, ran outside, cupped her hands, and started yelling. "Griffin! Your kite's about to fall in the drink! Get movin', will ya!"

Still in pain and holding his chest, Griffin turned to look back at Phoenix, forcing himself to smile, as though she could make out the expression on his face from that distance.

"Come on, team!" she yelled. "Fight, fight, fight!"

Griffin grinned at this, then looked toward his kite. The string was lax, and the kite was only about ten feet away from a watery grave.

Griffin took a step—and winced at the pain. He turned away so Phoenix couldn't see and touched his chest as though he could hold the pain and squeeze it to death.

Phoenix began a ridiculous parody of a cheerleader's dance. "Gimme a G! Gimme an R! Gimme an I!"

Griffin heard the cheer, gritted his teeth, and began running through the sand, his arms flailing away at the kite string, fighting to keep it up, forcing himself to ignore the pain, as Phoenix continued in the distance.

"Gimme an F! Gimme another F! Gimme an I! Gimme an N! What do they spell? GRIFFIN! Yeah, team!"

She jumped into the air, waving imaginary pom-

103

poms, leading the fantasy stadium crowd in the cheer.

Griffin ran hard, trying to keep the kite up.

Phoenix took another cheerleader's stance, grinning, starting to go into another funny chant, but she saw how hard he really was trying. Her arms slowly lowered from the start of her next cheer, and she sank to her knees in the sand. "Come on, Griffin," she whispered to him urgently. "You can do it."

The kite danced in the breeze, five feet above the waves.

Griffin ran, panting hard, as though trying to outrun the pain. His face was almost white, with beads of perspiration on his forehead. The sand was almost impossible to run in in his weak condition, but he kept trying, as though keeping this kite alive was the most important thing in the world.

Motionless, Phoenix just sat in the sand, speaking softly. "Please . . . you can do it . . ."

The kite was two feet above the water. A whitecap splashed a little water on it. The white cloth tail of the kite touched the water.

Griffin ran like hell, his face contorted.

Phoenix watched, mentally with him every step of the way.

The kite dipped a few more inches closer to the green sea, then the string tightened a little, the wind caught it, and it moved straight into the air, climbing —ten feet, fifteen, twenty, and higher!

Phoenix yelled and cavorted, doing cartwheels, throwing sand in the air; at that moment, she was the second happiest person in the world.

Griffin was first.

The pain in his face finally faded away and he continued running, working the kite string, controlling it, mastering it. He looked ecstatic, turned to wave at Phoenix, then noticed another person who was watching him.

The same expressionless old man who always wore the layers of clothes and a green scarf was nearby, seated on a bench. Only now, seeing Griffin, the old man smiled a wonderful smile. Slowly, almost majestically, the old man got to his feet and in a dignified way, as though he were at an opera, began to applaud Griffin.

Griffin smiled and waved at him, then back at Phoenix, who leaped in the air, waving back.

Griffin looked up at his kite.

In the bright sunlight, the beautiful yellow kite soared higher and higher against the blue sky, as though it were there to say.

Griffin, Phoenix, and several dozen other people watched from a high cliff one sunny afternoon as a young man soared overhead in a hang-glider. He gracefully caught each new air current, looking right at home in the sky. Passing seagulls never gave him a second glance.

Hang-gliders are the only Southern California phenomenon to have first appeared in Leonardo da Vinci's notebooks. His sketches were aerodynamically perfect, but he was born four hundred years before nylon and aluminum tubing.

Hang-gliders are twenty feet across, with a small seat-harness below, where a man sits, leaning into wind currents and shifting his weight, giving him the illusion that he has some control over his life as he sails off a cliff hundreds of yards above rocks and ocean.

As the young man approached another lower cliff, a sudden updraft made his hang-glider nosedive to the left, catching him in a down spiral.

The young man was ready, and somehow turned the near disaster into a beautiful 360-degree swoop, as though a final flourish, only seconds before he serenely sailed the hang-glider toward the sand, landed lightly on two feet, then routinely unstrapped himself.

Hundreds of yards above him, Phoenix finally exhaled, then looked over at Griffin.

No less scared, Griffin looked back at her from under the big yellow hang-glider where he was strapped in, about twenty feet from the edge of the cliff. Why should kites have all the fun, Griffin had asked himself, in a particularly *macho* moment.

A college kid walked past.

"Your turn in a minute, mister."

Griffin again studied the rigging, hefting the hang-glider which rested on his back, the nylon pounding in the strong wind.

"So what do you think, mister?" Phoenix said, half-yelling to be heard over the wind. "You still want to die with your boots on?"

Griffin didn't answer. His attention was on his own hang-glider. He glanced up at another in the sky, then back to his own, shifting his weight and doing some experimental steering moves. He looked so serious it was almost funny. Phoenix was amused until she went to the edge of the cliff and looked down.

It was a long, long way down to the rocks and sea below.

Phoenix stopped smiling.

She stood beside Griffin's hang-glider. Griffin continued to pretend he was actually soaring along, practicing his moves. Phoenix chewed on her lip a few moments, then leaned closer to him, half-yelling over the wind, half-whispering so other people wouldn't hear.

"Hey, something I meant to mention . . ." she said. "Do me a favor, will you?"

Griffin watched another kid sail off into space, catching an air current, but making a clumsy, dangerous turn.

"Let's don't talk about this a lot or anything," Phoenix continued, "but I want you to promise me that if I, you know, go first . . ."

Griffin suddenly turned and stared at her. She went right on.

". . . then don't you come to the hospital, funeral, or my grave. Okay?"

"Jesus Christ, Phoenix! *I'm* the one about to go off a cliff!"

"Let me finish. I just want to do this once. Whenever I think it's time, I'll just disappear, go to some hospital somewhere, and that's that. Don't look for me or anything. In fact, go back to your family. But let me do this the way I want."

A gust of wind almost lifted Griffin off the ground, scaring him.

"Goddammit, Phoenix! *I'm* the one about to fall off a cliff! I'll be dead in five minutes and you're standing there giving orders!"

"Okay, okay, I just wanted you to understand and do what I say about it. You hear me?"

He heard her. But he was busy lifting the hang-glider and carrying it toward the edge. Hang-gliders sail like an angel in the wind, but they're awkward on the ground, and the closer he got to the cliff's edge, the more the thirty-mile-an-hour updraft was buffeting the thin nylon. Phoenix walked beside him, helping him steady it.

Griffin stood two feet from the edge.

"Hey, you're not scared, are you?" Phoenix asked.

Wind hit the hang-glider, almost causing a premature takeoff.

"Well, yes," Griffin said, "I would say that I am a little scared, but as long as I'm here, I might as well try it."

"Next you're going to tell me the importance of living life to its fullest," she said dryly.

Then two college kids came over to Griffin.

"If you've got that twenty bucks and still want to," one of them said, "you're next."

The two kids took a position right on the edge of the cliff to help Griffin launch out into space.

"Ready?" one of them asked.

Griffin looked at Phoenix, who wanted to say something but knew she had to shut up. Griffin looked around, then up at the sky, then took a deep breath.

"Yeah, I'm ready," he said, unstrapping himself. "I'm ready for a beer and a hamburger. C'mon, Phoenix." Griffin climbed out of the rigging, Phoenix looked happy, wisely saying nothing, and the two of them hurried away, leaving two college kids staring after them with their mouths open.

They were sitting in the car in the parking lot of an all-night supermarket, making a quick shopping list they'd try to stick to, when Phoenix noticed Griffin wasn't paying attention.

"Hey," she said, "I'm not any more excited about

discussing pork chops than you are, but I thought we were going to try to save our money for other things and you said we should—"

"I know," Griffin said, with a strange smile on his face. "I was just thinking about something else." Excitedly, he grabbed her elbow. "I'm getting this really crazy idea. I mean it's really way out, so it's either a *terrible* idea or it's *brilliant,* and—"

"What? What is it?" Griffin's face was really lit up, and Phoenix wanted to join his excitement.

"Well," Griffin said, "I just now thought of it, and I haven't thought it out or anything, but—"

"Tell me, Griffin!"

"Let's have a baby!"

Phoenix looked at him like he was crazy.

"I know neither one of us will be around to raise it, but don't you find something beautiful about a child knowing that the last thing his two parents chose to do before they died was to create a new life? I mean, we can't do anything about ourselves, but we just might have time to come up with this brand new person! My brother George might raise her for us, and he could tell her about us and why we had her, or we could leave some letters for her when the kid's old enough or something!"

Phoenix still couldn't believe this whole conversation.

"Griffin," she finally said, carefully picking her words. "Production takes nine months, and lately I haven't really been planning that far ahead."

"Hey, I know," he said softly. "It might be a race against time, but hell, Phoenix, who's more competitive than we are? And I know it might sound strange for me to talk about having a kid when I haven't exactly been . . ." he dropped his eyes, unconsciously ". . . the most virile, red-blooded—"

"Stop it."

"Anyway, one way or another, we could get you pregnant by me. And there *might* be time. Don't you think it's a wonderful idea? I mean, it's crazy, but she would know that we wanted her to, you know, go on and live *for* us . . ."

"What's this *she* business? You're trying to act like you'd want a girl instead of a little Griffin?"

He looked her right in the eye. "I'd want someone exactly like you . . . that was mine, too."

He meant it; what he wanted was a little Phoenix. She looked away, out toward the parking lot, where people were shoving shopping carts toward their cars. He couldn't see her face.

"Let me think. Jesus, Griffin . . . go shopping or something." She spoke quietly and didn't turn back around.

He nodded and hurried toward the all-night supermarket, glancing at the list. He flew through the market, quickly getting what they needed, hurried back out to the car, set the stuff in the back seat, got in, and didn't say anything. He just waited.

Phoenix was composed and ready.

"Griffin . . . on a philosophical level, it *is* a terrific idea, and maybe there *would* be time, and I've always wanted a child . . . but there's one other, very down-to-earth thing that I gotta tell you honestly that I've just realized." He waited. "If I've only got less than a year to live . . . I don't want to live it pregnant."

"Oh," Griffin said.

The next day at dinner, Griffin apologized like crazy for even mentioning the baby idea, saying it was stupid and insensitive of him. Phoenix smiled and said it was a beautiful idea and she was prouder of him than ever for having the idea, and she kissed him. He tasted like pork chops.

AUGUST, 1975—LOS ANGELES

One afternoon, Griffin told Phoenix he was going to do their laundry, headed for the Laundromat, left their stuff whirling around, and hurried for his secret appointment.

"Remission is impossible at this point, you know that, don't you?"

The doctor was a kind, smiling man.

"Just give me something for pain," Griffin said.

The doctor nodded, then turned to his bookshelf. "About the only other thing I can do for you, since you refuse hospitalization, is to lend you some books that might help . . ."

Books, Griffin thought, shaking his head in amusement. Take two volumes and call me in the morning.

It was late at night, and Griffin stood and stared out of his bedroom window. He lived right by the ocean, but this particular window faced an alley.

"I smoke too much," Phoenix said from the bed, her tone sounding a little too light. "Bad for my health."

She looked up at Griffin, who still just stood there in his underwear, staring away from her.

"Hey," she said, "would you stop? It doesn't matter."

"It does matter, and you know it." That's all he needed, he thought to himself, being told that sex doesn't matter. It ain't everything but, Jesus . . .

"For us, maybe that's all that *does* matter." He paused, then added quietly, "I went to a shrink."

"Why didn't you tell me?"

"I'm telling you. It took the monkey half an hour just to get over the novelty of the situation. He finally allowed as how I probably can't achieve such a life-affirming act when I'm subconsciously always aware that we're both full of death."

"What did it cost to learn that?"

"Thirty-five bucks."

Griffin sighed happily and patted his stomach. From across the dinner, Phoenix smiled and held up a big bowl.

"More?"

Griffin shook his head. They were at home and Phoenix had just finished eating—bone steaks, twice-baked potatoes, French bread, and red wine.

Griffin belched.

"It's my own recipe."

Griffin stared down at his plate.

"It's interesting, psychologically, that the moment you've decided you're full," Griffin said, "the remains of a delicious dinner change, in that split second, to garbage."

"What you mean is, you're not anxious to do the dishes."

"Right."

"You know it's your turn."

"I hate doing dishes."

"Tell you what. You wash and you dry."

"What will you do?"

"I'll watch. I did them last night, remember?"

"I *despise* doing dishes."

"Life can be cruel."

He looked at her, then down at the dishes again. Then he suddenly leaned across the table, looking very serious.

"Look, let's just leave the dishes like they are and go to a show or something. The magic elves will do them—"

"Griffin."

"No, I meant it. Magic elves live under the sink, and they come out at night, when everyone's asleep, and do all the dishes—"

"Okay, I'll help you—"

"You don't believe me, do you? But it's true! They'll do the dishes with cute little invisible wash-cloths and everything—look!" He suddenly pointed across the room. "There goes one now! Ah, you missed him. A little teeny magic elf ran across the room and under the sofa . . ."

Phoenix stared up at the ceiling and softly drummed her fingers on the table.

"You couldn't see him because you don't *believe*," Griffin said, in an accusing tone.

"These are my dishes and stuff, right?" Phoenix said, suddenly, getting to her feet and walking into the kitchen. "I mean, these are the ones I brought from my apartment with me, aren't they?"

"Yeah," Griffin said, puzzled. "Why?"

Phoenix returned with a large empty metal waste-

111

basket and set it beside the table. She was smiling.

"You aren't the only who hates doing dishes, you know."

Phoenix picked up her plate, complete with knife and fork, and her half-finished glass of wine, held them high in the air above the wastebasket, smiled, and let them drop.

CRASH!

Griffin stared at her.

"Always wanted to do this with the dirty dishes," Phoenix said, reaching for her salad bowl and the bottle of salad dressing.

"This is silly," Griffin said, grinning in spite of himself. "We'll just have to buy all new stuff tomorrow."

"We sure will," Phoenix said, and let go of the bottle and bowl. CRASH! Thousand Island dressing, glass, and lettuce now covered the bottom of the wastebasket.

Griffin picked up his plate and held it in the air. CRASH!

Suddenly, both Griffin and Phoenix started grabbing things as fast as they could. Silverware, salt and pepper shakers, steak sauce, flower and vase, a candle, butter dish, everything went. CRASH! CRASH! CRASH! Then Phoenix quickly stuffed the tablecloth in the wastebasket, and Griffin took the trash out and emptied it.

Since the dishes were done, they went to the double feature.

FALL-WINTER, 1975—LOS ANGELES

Time passed, sometimes rushing, sometimes in a wonderful slow motion. Griffin and Phoenix would have been the last ones to know how many days were going by; they never had any truck with schedules or clocks or people who did. They lived their own crazy nonroutine, starting one day before dawn to get the most out of it, or sleeping until late afternoon, eating breakfast at sundown, and playing all night. They were explorers: venturing into new territory with each other, discovering what might really be done with something as precious as a minute. They were together and they were happy, and it continually amazed them how much life you could squeeze out of a Tuesday night with only love and a couple of dollars.

Griffin and Phoenix knew they'd go back to reality soon enough; they were just waiting for the off-season, when it wouldn't be so crowded.

Phoenix sat on the sand near the ocean waves, facing a small fire and a big sunset. Two hot dogs were stuck on a bent coat-hanger which she held over the flames. Around her were hot-dog buns, mustard, and paper plates.

Griffin trudged through the sand thirty feet behind her, carrying a big, cold magnum of champagne and some Dixie cups. Then he stopped and smiled to himself in an evil way, quietly set the cups down, unpeeled the wrapper on the top, aimed the bottle toward Phoenix, and began to ease the explosive plastic cork.

The beach was empty. It was too cool and windy an evening for most people, so Griffin had a clear line of vision. He studied the angle, wind velocity, estimated the point of impact, which he hoped would be the top of her head, and finally popped the cork.

Phoenix heard the sound, then suddenly saw the cork land in the sand two feet away from her. She picked it up, turned and made a face at him, grinning, then turned back to the fire.

"Come on, your hot dog's about done," she said.

Shrugging, sorry he'd missed her, Griffin picked up the paper cups and continued walking through the sand.

He was about fifteen feet away from her, directly behind her, when the pain slammed through his chest.

He dropped the bottle and cups, groped for his chest, and staggered a few feet to one side, never having felt anything like it before in his life. Through blurred eyes, he watched Phoenix closely, knowing she might turn around at any moment. She didn't know

113

about his pain. He wanted to keep it that way. He didn't take his eyes off her.

Phoenix hummed to herself and played with the hot dog on the coat-hanger, letting it dance in and out of the flames.

Chapter Ten

Fighting to keep his balance, Griffin tried to think about something else, anything else. Random thoughts went through his mind, linked together by dull, steady waves of pain.

Griffin remembered an article he wished he'd never read. It explained a unique way Eskimos have of hunting polar bears.

They take a small, curved bone, work on it until it's razor-sharp, then bend it back as far as possible, like a coiled spring, and freeze it in that position. The chunk of ice is set inside a seal carcass. A bear comes loping along, eats it, licks his lips, and happily goes about his daily polar bear business: slide down a few ice floes, chase his favorite lady polar bear, maybe knock in a few igloos, then go carousing that night with a few of the guys. The Eskimos patiently stalk the bear wherever he goes. They keep a safe distance, not having to keep the bear in sight. They know they will be able to hear it, even from a great distance, the moment the bear's internal body heat melts the ball of ice.

Griffin fumbled in his pocket for his pain pills and washed a couple of them down with champagne, straight from the bottle, carefully watching Phoenix. He knew his face was white, his balance off, his hands shaking. He turned and forced himself to walk slowly back the way he'd come.

Phoenix turned around.

"Hey!" she yelled, smiling. "Just because you missed me is no reason to go off and sulk!"

Not turning his head, Griffin felt the pain begin to recede, but he needed a few more moments. Sometimes it faded back into a manageable level as quickly as it had flared up.

"Nap . . ." he tried to yell, but it came out a whisper. He yelled louder. "Napkins . . ."

"We got some here, remember? Come on, will ya? Bring on the booze, goddammit!" She enjoyed her lady-like behavior immensely.

As Griffin slowly turned and started walking back, he began feeling better. Walking helped, or maybe activity got his mind off the pain for a few moments. Anyway, he was feeling better. Fucking Eskimos, he thought, and sat down by Phoenix, forcing a smile.

"Just my luck. Turns out you're a wino."

"You're the one who said we needed a magnum to go with a couple of hot dogs," she said, pouring them each a drink.

"Hey," Griffin said, after a long sip. "I want to give you a present."

"A present?"

"Yeah."

"Why?"

Griffin took another drink, looked at the sunset, then smiled at Phoenix.

"Because you gave me a train."

He put some mustard on his hot dog and took a bite.

"What can I give you that you always used to want?" he asked.

"I don't know." She thought a moment. "How about one single perfect Venus fly-trap?"

"Come on."

"Well, I don't know. I always wanted the Pyramids to get a chance to see me."

Griffin's voice got serious for a moment. "I wish we had the money."

"I know. Too bad money actually can buy happiness."

"What about cheap thrills?"

"Hey, I know!" She laughed.

116

"What?"

"Well, I just thought of something. In high school, I was always on the fringes of being in the 'popular crowd'—but never made it. I tried out every year for cheerleader. Never made it. In my home room every year, I always ran for Student Council representative."

"Never made it."

"Right. My whole life I've been trying out for the lead in the school play, and I've always ended up painting scenery."

She paused and took a big bite of hot dog, making the rest of what she said sound like Latin. "Anyway, there was this one last thing that really killed me because I didn't get to do it."

"Phoenix, you're speaking Hot Dog. I can't understand you."

Big drink. Big swallow.

"Look, it's really silly," she said.

"What is it?"

"Well . . ."

"Tell me."

She told him.

Against the night sky, the gigantic water tower rose nearly two hundred feet above their heads. There were several lights at the top, a tiny catwalk, and a ladder extending all the way down one side, as though anyone would actually try to climb up the damn thing.

Griffin and Phoenix peered up at the water tower from behind some bushes. They wore old, dark clothes and carried a big can of paint and two big house-painting brushes.

"You didn't happen to ask your high school cronies how they got up there, did you?" he asked her.

"Haven't you done this, either?" Phoenix asked, surprised. "You seem like the type."

"Only lately. In those days, I used to worry about things like getting caught, or I'd hesitate, or—"

"You mean you were chicken."

"Well, I wasn't going to say it quite that way, but that does sort of capture the essence of the thing."

117

Phoenix flicked on a flashlight and they started toward the water tower.

Their first problem was a high, barbed-wire fence that surrounded the base of the tower. Griffin took off his jacket and covered some of the barbs and they climbed over, handing the brushes and paint can to each other.

Then there was the ladder.

The bottom rung was nine feet off the ground, forcing Griffin and Phoenix to do a little Marx Brothers routine as she climbed up on his shoulders, while trying to keep the can of paint slung over her shoulder, maintaining her balance by putting her foot in Griffin's face.

She got her hands on the rung finally, but couldn't get much higher.

"I don't know if I can get up here," Phoenix said.

"It's your water tower, lady."

Using physical strength she wasn't used to using, Phoenix gritted her teeth and pulled herself up, catching a knee in the bottom rung, finally pulling herself on up. She hooked an elbow around a rung, and watched Griffin.

He backed up, ran, and made a rather glorious leap and a one-hand stab at the bottom rung, then swung himself on up.

One hundred and sixty feet later, they didn't feel exactly glorious, just scared and tired. Strong gusts of wind made the tiny ladder rattle dangerously. It occurred to Phoenix that the ladder was probably designed just to hold the weight of only one person.

"If I mention my fear of heights," Phoenix yelled down to Griffin, who was just behind her, "you'll probably just tell me not to look down, right?"

"Look!" Griffin pointed above them.

Phoenix turned, but all she saw was the surface of the top of the tower, which was a uniform gray color.

"Not a single kid has climbed up here and painted anything!" Griffin said.

Phoenix was clinging to the ladder, her hair blown in the wind, completely petrified. "Yeah," she mumbled to herself, "kids today just don't know how to have fun."

They finally reached the narrow catwalk at the top of the tower. The wind pounded away at them, but they were glad to be done with that ladder. They looked out at the beautiful city lights all around them before turning on the flashlight and opening the can of paint.

At the base of the water tower, unnoticed by Griffin and Phoenix, a police car slowly pulled in, stopped with lights off, and waited.

Using broad, confident strokes, Phoenix finished painting "CLASS OF '59" in huge Day-Glo orange letters about eight feet high, obviously enjoying herself. Griffin, also having fun, scampered around the edge of the tower carrying a wet paintbrush, dipping his brush into the can of paint, then quickly went back just out of Phoenix's sight, to her right.

"Hey, what are you doing around there?" she had to yell over the wind.

"You aren't the only one who's always wanted to do this, you know!" Griffin yelled, from the side.

Phoenix took a step back to admire her accomplishment. She was careful not to take two steps back. She looked pleased with herself.

"Class of '59 . . . just imagine the irritated look on the face of some city maintenance man. He'll have to climb up here and cover this up with dull gray paint when he could be home watching the ballgame."

Griffin walked around the edge of the tower, casually tossing his paintbrush off into the night. They looked at each other, feeling pretty cocky. Phoenix gave Griffin a big kiss, then looked at him, positively radiant.

"My very own water tower," she said. "Just what I've always wanted."

Griffin smiled back.

"This is all very nice, except that we have to climb back down . . ."

He glanced down.

"Perhaps the power of prayer can . . . uh-oh." Griffin suddenly looked unhappy. Phoenix looked down.

119

They both saw the tiny police car below. From their height, it looked like a toy. Inside, they realized, was a little toy policeman who would take them to a cute little toy jail.

Phoenix led the slow descent down the ladder.

"You don't suppose that cop will believe sleepwalking, do you?" Griffin asked.

"I'm just glad it's not the S.W.A.T. truck," she said. "They could pick us off easy—"

Her foot suddenly slipped off the rung, twisting inside.

She began to fall.

She screamed, grabbing out with one hand.

Griffin quickly moved toward her.

Her right hand missed the ladder and her body began falling away from the ladder, but her left hand caught a rung.

"Hang on!" Griffin yelled, grabbing her sweatshirt, nearly falling himself.

"Griffin!" she yelled, frightened.

"You'll be okay! Get your grip there! Now try to get your footing . . ."

His knuckles turned white, where he held onto her sweatshirt.

"Come on! Get your footing! Have you got it?"

He held the twisted-up sweatshirt tightly, but his other hand was starting to slip.

Phoenix managed to scramble her foot onto a rung and got both hands back in place.

"I got it."

Griffin slowly let go of her and got a better grip himself. Finally secure, they both just leaned against the ladder and rested for a few moments.

"Jesus . . ." she finally said.

"You're okay now."

"I'm sorry, Griffin. I could have taken you with me."

"Yeah. Be awful if we fell and got killed, wouldn't it?"

"Be a damned shame," she said, and they both began laughing.

Twenty minutes later, they dropped from the last

rung of the ladder into the long arms of the law.

A flashlight beam hit them in the eyes.

"All right! Step over here. Now." The policeman's voice startled them, even though they knew he was there. Using the jacket to cover the barbed wire, Griffin and Phoenix started climbing over the fence as the cop walked up, still shining the light in their faces, his gun drawn.

"Just get over that fence and come here. You want to tell me what you were doing up there before I read you your rights?"

"We were recapturing our lost youth, officer," Griffin said, with a straight face.

Griffin and Phoenix finished climbing the fence and stood before the policeman.

"You folks been drinking, have you?"

"Oh, no, sir," Griffin said, then suddenly cupped his hand and yelled up to the top of the tower. "Stay there, Mom! Cops!"

The cop whirled around, aiming his flashlight and gun toward the top of the water tower.

"Anybody else up there, you get on down, and I mean now!"

The cop studied the silent, dark water tower. The only thing unusual up there was "CLASS OF '59" in huge letters.

Actually, the cop didn't mind very much what they had done, personally. He had graduated in '59 himself. But he decided it was his duty to arrest them anyway; a man's gotta do what a man's gotta do. He turned back to Griffin and Phoenix.

They weren't there any more.

Holding hands, they raced through the trees and bushes in the field beside the water tower. Phoenix laughed so hard she almost couldn't run.

The angry cop began chasing them through the undergrowth.

They had about a forty-foot head start, but it wouldn't be enough. Before long, Phoenix thought, we'll be wearing bracelets. Heading for the slammer. Then she saw a small hole in some thick bushes and dived through it, dragging Griffin with her.

Phoenix had finally stopped giggling, but Griffin was still about to break up. They could hear the sound of the cop's footsteps getting closer. Griffin tickled Phoenix. She silently pounded on him, trying to get him to stop. The only sound was leaves rustling as Phoenix tried to squirm away from him but couldn't.

The cop ran up next to where they lay hiding. They could see his shoes and hear him pant as he paused for a moment, shining his light around.

"Come back here, damn you!" yelled the cop into the night. He hurried on, leaving Griffin and Phoenix nearly in hysterics.

As the cop's footsteps faded away, they finally stopped giggling and stretched out on their backs, getting comfortable while waiting for the cop to return and drive away. Then Phoenix, still giggling, leaned over and gave Griffin a quick kiss. He gave her a quick kiss back.

Then they stopped smiling and started kissing each other most seriously.

They held each other and kissed again and hugged each other tighter and tighter, kissing, caressing, getting more and more excited. Griffin kissed her lips, her face, her neck, pulling her clothes aside, as she clawed at his back, her hands on his shoulders and chest and arms and waist and legs . . .

Their clothes, all their clothes, were soon tossed aside and forgotten, and the only sound in the field was the rustling of leaves and happy groaning and the wind in the trees.

That night, home in bed, they made love again.

The next morning, they woke up happy and made love again.

That afternoon . . .

"First I can't get you started, then I can't get you stopped."

Phoenix, sweating and out of breath, rolled over on her side and leaned up on one elbow.

"Gripe, gripe, gripe," Griffin said, watching how the late afternoon sunlight made stripes on her beautiful nude body.

"Believe me," she said, "I'm not griping." She

smiled in a very sexy way and slowly touched his face with her fingertips. He looked at her and smiled. He was a little proud of himself, and with her he could let his pride show.

Phoenix let her fingertips slowly move down his face and neck to his chest muscles, lightly touching them. His chest glistened with sweat from both of them. She tried to think of what the right word was for what she had discovered about his body, how it felt to her, when they had both shaken from it, and she realized that her happy discovery was in the *power* in his body, power and strength and gentleness.

She lay on her back and stretched and smiled.

"Hey," she finally said, being serious. "I feel . . . really *good*. I don't mean just after-making-love good, I mean . . ." She tried to think of the words, and couldn't.

"Do you know how happy I am right now?" It wasn't a rhetorical question. She was really asking.

Griffin thought about it. He knew how happy *he* was, and it really wasn't just the sex. And he realized that was what she meant, too.

"Yeah. I know."

Phoenix realized that he did know; she leaned over and kissed him.

They were at a pizza parlor, getting their weekly pepperoni fix. Griffin ordered a big one to go, while Phoenix went into the ladies' room.

There was a pretty, shy girl about nineteen, crying.

"You okay, honey?" Phoenix asked.

"Yeah," the girl sobbed, turning away, embarrassed at her crying. There was a pretty, old-fashioned quality about her; she was the only woman under thirty in the Pacific Time Zone who still wore a bra.

"I just got stood up," the girl said, composing herself. "I really liked the guy."

Phoenix awkwardly patted the girl on the shoulder.

"Listen," she said, "I'm older than you. Happens all the time. Why, I've been stood up in my time by Deputy City Attorneys, forest rangers, heart specialists, aluminum-siding salesmen, you name it. All on the same night, too."

Phoenix continued.

"Want to know one thing you can always count on with men?"

"Yes."

"I would, too."

The girl smiled back, almost laughing in spite of herself.

Griffin and Phoenix were walking down the street, trying to finish their pizza ten minutes later, when a tall young man emerged from the bus station. He was good-looking, had a friendly smile, and carried a big suitcase.

"Excuse me," he said, "but could you tell me which way Hollywood and Vine is?"

"Couple of blocks that way," Griffin said, "but it's not worth the walk."

"Hope you're not expecting the ole 'magic of Hollywood,'" Phoenix said dryly. "It's just a street sign."

The young man smiled good-naturedly.

"Oh, I just want to see some place famous before I get a room tonight."

"You ever been here before?" Griffin asked him, his mouth full of pizza.

"Nope. Just got in from Tulsa two minutes ago. But this is my home now!"

He looked around, his eyes full of wonder.

"Sure is exciting, isn't it?"

Instinctively, Griffin and Phoenix glanced around and saw absolutely nothing exciting, but realized how the young man must be seeing things.

"Yeah," Griffin said, nodding. "Yeah, it *is* exciting. Got any friends here? Family? Want some pizza?"

"No, thanks. Nope, nobody yet, but I'll meet people. Well, thanks a lot!"

With long, confident strides, he was off, entering his new world.

"So long!" Griffin and Phoenix yelled. "Good luck!"

"You forget sometimes there are still nice people in the world . . ." Griffin said.

"Yeah, it's like that girl back at the pizza place I told you about; she was really sweet . . ."

Then Griffin and Phoenix slowly looked at each other, having the same idea at the same time.

Hollywood and Vine today is only a drugstore and nostalgia, but the young man from Tulsa gawked a lot, still holding his suitcase when Griffin finally spotted him. He ran over to him and began talking fast.

A few minutes later, Phoenix ran up with the shy, attractive young woman from the pizza place.

"Hi! Well, here we are," Phoenix said. "Shirley, this is Griffin."

"Hi ya, Shirley," Griffin said, with a big smile. "I'd like to introduce you to my old friend . . ." He turned to the young man. "What's your name?"

"Chuck."

"Right, Chuck," Griffin said, hurrying on. "Shirley, Chuck. Chuck, Shirley. Chuck and I went to different schools together."

"Right now, here's the thing," Phoenix said, jumping in. "Chuck's new in town, doesn't know anyone, and he's real nice, and Shirley knows L.A. and she's real nice, and we're all real nice, and Griffin and I are getting the hell out of here."

She grabbed Griffin and they headed off into the night, waving to the confused couple. "I know you two got a lot to talk about," Griffin yelled. " 'Bye."

Chuck and Shirley smiled at each other shyly and began talking.

Griffin and Phoenix glanced back, exchanged looks, and began singing an offbeat, exaggerated version of "Hooray for Hollywood," and half-walked, half-danced off down the street.

Chapter Eleven

Some time later, in the middle of the night, it suddenly happened.

There was no warning. They had spent a fairly routine day, which meant that there wasn't any routine at all, yet nothing in particular caused it. It was everything in particular.

One moment, Griffin and Phoenix were sleeping in the bed peacefully. The bedroom curtains stirred a little from the breeze, and shadows played on the wall in the light from a nearby street light. The ocean waves, a hundred yards away, slapped against the shore a little more gently than usual. Everything was still and quiet.

Phoenix screamed at the top of her lungs.

She rolled out of bed, a look of pure fear on her face, scrambling, more like an animal than a human being, to a corner of the room, where she crouched whimpering, now completely awake, which didn't help because being awake was worse.

Griffin, looking around wildly to see what had happened, crawled across the bed and onto the floor to the corner where Phoenix stared at him as though she didn't know how or what he was.

"Phoenix?" He spoke softly. "Hey, it's okay . . . everything's all right . . ." He slowly touched her shoulder to draw her near.

Phoenix exploded at the touch, screaming, running

across the room toward the wall, not even seeing it.

She crashed into the wall, hitting her forehead and arm, but she didn't feel anything except the private terror she was trying to outrun. Moaning, she turned and ran in a different direction at top speed.

Griffin almost had her, but she screamed and spun around with crazy, jerky motions, tearing through the shadows to the closet door, pulled at the doorknob, but couldn't get it open, and began pounding on the door, wanting in, wanting out, yelling, crying, panting.

Griffin grabbed her shoulders, shaking her.

"Phoenix!"

"No! NO!" she screamed, sliding out of his reach, scrambling across the floor to a new corner by the dresser, whimpering, terrified, wanting so very much to wake up one more time.

Griffin caught her again as she curled into a little ball in the corner, screaming up toward the roof. "It's not fair! IT'S NOT FAIR!"

She screamed, and her arms flailed away at real or imagined horrors, fists that in fact only met Griffin's face. He didn't even try to shield himself, but simply put his arms around her tightly, holding her, and her yelling finally diminished into sobs.

"No . . . it's not fair . . ."

Griffin curled up beside her and pulled her toward him against his chest, his arms around her. He rocked her gently back and forth, soothing her like a child, speaking softly as she sobbed, her breath coming in big gasps. He didn't try to tell her everything would be all right; he simply held her.

"No, it's not fair . . ." Griffin softly murmured over and over. "It's not fair at all . . ."

He held her tightly, and she held him, and they rocked back and forth very closely in the shadowy corner of the dark room.

The bedroom curtains stirred a little from the breeze, and outside the ocean waves slapped against the shore a little more gently than usual.

The morning fog decided to stick around through

the afternoon, so Griffin and Phoenix stayed inside all day playing Scrabble, until she won her third game by playing "quartz" on a triple-word-score.

"Well, just remember, Griffy ol' boy, it ain't who wins or loses," Phoenix said triumphantly, "it's how you dig the dug-out."

"This time we're going to play a new version, one I can win. You ever played Dirty Scrabble?"

"No, and you haven't, either, you just made it up—"

"Dirty Scrabble," Griffin interrupted, making it up, "can be played using either college or pro rules. See, you can only play dirty words on the Scrabble board, and the first person to giggle loses. How about a game?"

"I should warn you. You could lose at this one, too."

"Oh. Well, then, how about a fast game of Strip Scrabble?"

"What?"

"You know, Strip Scrabble," Griffin said matter-of-factly, making it up as fast as he could. "You've heard of Strip Poker? Well, in Strip Scrabble, see, even if you lose, you win."

Griffin had lost a sock, a shoe, and his belt when they heard a knock at the door.

A very pretty little girl about six years old with brown hair stood there, nervously fiddling with her dress and holding a piece of paper. She had big eyes and looked up at Griffin, who smiled at her.

"Are you the man with the kite?" she asked him.

"Am I . . . ?" Griffin was confused. "Well, yes, I guess I'm the man with the kite . . ."

The little girl took a deep breath, and her recitation began.

"My grampa says that if you're the man with the kite that he . . . uh . . . that he . . ."

"Hello, my name's Sarah," Phoenix said, smiling and bending close. "What's your name?"

"Sharon Elizabeth." She took a deep breath and had to start over.

"My grampa says that if you're the man with the

kite that he wants you to come to his birthday party, and this is the address."

She suddenly thrust the piece of paper at Griffin, then ran away, her little feet clumping off. The door still open, Griffin and Phoenix just looked at each other. Then the sound of small, clumping feet returned and the little girl suddenly appeared again, looked up at Phoenix, and yelled loudly, excited at her first executive decision.

"You can come, too!" And then she was gone.

It was an old-fashioned family gathering in a big old comfortable home, with forty or fifty people wandering around, most of them related. There was laughter, drinks, music, and enough food to feed a rather large army.

Griffin and Phoenix came up to the door, which was open, and peered inside. They were puzzled about just who was throwing this bash and why they were invited, but after Griffin lost two games of Strip Scrabble, with a charming intermission after each game, they dressed up and decided to go to the address on the piece of paper. The old home was only a few blocks from the beach.

Griffin and Phoenix were a little hesitant about entering, even though smiling people were streaming in and out, until Griffin saw a familiar face.

Through the crowd, he saw the same old man on the beach who always wore a green scarf, and the old man saw him. The old man's face immediately lit up, and he made an expansive gesture for them to enter his home. Griffin and Phoenix could feel the welcome all the way across the room, waved back, and joined the merry occasion.

Large families usually see each other only at weddings and funerals, when they say how it's too bad they only see each other at weddings and funerals. But this seemed to be a family that had the good sense to gather when they were all healthy and happy and seemed to enjoy a good time together.

Like the way they got the old man to sing.

Three people ushered him over by the piano, and a middle-aged niece with horn-rimmed glasses sat down and began to play "Loch Lomond." The gathering quieted down. The old man, whose name turned out to be Mr. MacDougall, took a sip of water and slowly began to sing, looking all the while at his gray-haired, smiling wife of the last fifty-eight years.

"When me and my true love . . . forever shall roam . . . on the bonnie, bonnie banks of Loch Lomond . . ."

His singing voice was a little shaky, but there was dignity in his manner and love in his eyes and, when he finished, everyone applauded. Especially Griffin, who proudly wore the green scarf Mr. MacDougall had given him.

Mr. MacDougall opened his presents with the usual noisy fun that goes with well-meant, inappropriate gifts. His wife helped him with the ribbons and paper. Phoenix looked around to see where Griffin had disappeared to, then glanced out of the window and saw him.

Griffin ran in, panting, carrying a brand new kite and string, and went over and gave it to Mr. Mac-Dougall, who shook Griffin's hand in true appreciation.

When Griffin went over to join Phoenix, she pulled him around a corner through a hallway into a bedroom, where a bed was piled high with jackets and coats, for a brief moment of privacy.

Phoenix practically pinned Griffin to the wall with a big kiss.

"Wow . . ." Griffin said. "Something special?"

"Yeah. You."

Just then a man hurried into the room, awkwardly interrupting them. He smiled sheepishly, tried to find his coat, and left.

"Phoenix, have I mentioned how much I like you?" Griffin asked her, as they started to rejoin the others. "I don't mean love you. You already know that. But I *like* you a lot, too."

Phoenix just looked at him, happy, delighted, amazed, contented. Arm in arm, they went back to the party.

Mr. MacDougall was finishing opening his presents and many of his relatives started yelling, "Speech, speech!" It got quiet, and the old gentleman cleared his throat.

"I am eighty years old today—" He was interrupted by applause. "And I have been asked to say something on this occasion. But to have friends and family such as you . . . speaks for itself." It was totally quiet in the large old home, and he spoke slowly and simply. "You are the good that my life has been . . . you . . . and my Anna." He motioned for his wife.

Hesitantly, almost shyly, she joined him. Gently, he kissed her, then after a moment of silence, everyone converged on them with handshakes and kisses.

Griffin and Phoenix joined in the applause, but they could not at that moment look at each other, not after seeing two people who had grown old together.

Someone found some 1940s waltz music. Phoenix walked across the room to ask Mr. MacDougall to dance, making a mental note to keep the dance steps simple and not to tire out the old gentleman. Mr. Mac-Dougall, pleased at being asked by such a lovely young woman, made a slight bow, then swept her off her feet and onto the impromptu dance floor, leading her gracefully across the room, making it obvious that he was a very accomplished dancer, to everyone's delight. She gave the old man a kiss, which he loved.

Watching all this, Griffin then went over to the fattest, least attractive woman and asked her to dance. Flustered, she accepted, and soon everyone else joined them on the dance floor.

Later, a nice woman about forty years old came over to Griffin and Phoenix.

"We're all happy you both could come today," she said. "When Grampa said he wanted you here, I asked him about you, and he would only say that you are a 'man of accomplishment.' " In a friendly way, the woman was openly puzzled about this and smiled and waited for an explanation. But Griffin just smiled back and rocked back on his heels, proudly.

"A man of accomplishment . . . well, ma'am, that's me," he said, mysteriously.

The woman looked to Phoenix for an explanation. But she just slipped her arm through his and said, "That's him."

They both just smiled at the woman, who vaguely smiled back and wandered away, more confused than ever.

Just before they left, Phoenix noticed two old men, checker-playing cronies of Mr. MacDougall's, trying to get close enough to a punchbowl to spike it with a bottle wrapped in a brown paper bag. The large matronly woman stood by the punchbowl, however, like a guard.

Phoenix went over to distract her with conversation. She walked up to the woman, causing her to half-turn away from the punchbowl.

"Excuse me," Phoenix said, "but hasn't it been a lovely party?"

"Why yes, it has," said the woman.

"By the way, did you know that when Cortez first came to North America, that if his cattle had wandered away from him instead of his horses, the Indians would have ridden cows?"

The matronly woman started to reply, then realized she didn't know what to say. The two old codgers were sneaking up to the bowl, quietly cackling, getting the bottle ready.

"I was just reading the other day," Phoenix said, quickly going on, before the woman turned back around. "Did you know that there's enough lime in the human body to whitewash a chicken coop?"

A quart of gin was being poured into the punchbowl silently, as the matronly woman opened her mouth to speak, but her mouth just opened and closed a few times. The old codgers quickly retreated, mission accomplished, so Phoenix just smiled and wandered off to find Griffin, who was probably wearing a lampshade somewhere. The matronly woman just stared after Phoenix, then fixed herself a big glass of punch.

Phoenix walked past the two old codgers. The first old guy winked at her. Phoenix winked back. The second one pinched her. She jumped and tried to look

133

indignant but, actually, she wouldn't have had it any other way.

JANUARY, 1976—LOS ANGELES

Griffin charged into the costume rental shop, carrying two boxes. He and Phoenix had worn the costumes the day before while visiting maternity stores and shopping for cribs.

"These priest and nun outfits worked great," Griffin told the man behind the counter. Just then, Griffin's face went white, and he held his chest and leaned forward on the counter.

"Hey, you all right, buddy?"

Griffin nodded his head yes, fumbled in his pocket for his pills, tossed a couple down, and swallowed them dry. God must not have thought that priest business was very funny, he thought. After a moment, he stood up straight, still breathing a little heavily. That pain hadn't been bad at all, and yet he knew that before long, there would be no more pain.

"Sure you okay?"

Griffin nodded.

"Tell you what," the man behind the counter said. "You got these costumes back early, so I'll give you a discount on a couple more."

"No, I don't think we need any more," Griffin said, shaking his head no, until he noticed the two large, absolutely insane gorilla costumes in the corner.

Twenty minutes later, he happily got out of his car, carrying the new costume boxes under his arm and headed toward his apartment. He put one of the gorilla masks on his head, humming to himself.

He burst into his apartment, roaring and pounding his chest, trying to scare the royal bejesus out of ol' Phoenix. But she wasn't in the living room.

"Hey, I got a new sexy nightgown for you," he yelled, hurrying into the bedroom. But she wasn't there. He went back into the living room.

Then he saw it.

He stopped in the doorway, staring at it, slowly pulling his gorilla mask off. Across the room, there was a small note pinned to the chair.

Phoenix was a note-writer, he knew that. She'd left notes all the time. Once, he'd found one in the freezer. But somehow he knew this one was different, and somehow he knew he didn't want to go over and read it. His hand shook a little as he read:

> It's time for you to go spend time with your family. Tell your kids to catch their freight trains. I've been in a lot of pain but haven't wanted you to know. Remember what you promised about not looking for me. God, I love you.
>
> PHOENIX

Stunned and shaken, not knowing what to do, Griffin turned and looked around, knowing she wouldn't be there. He called out to her in a whisper.

"Sarah . . ."

He slowly sank into the chair, his head bowed, and began hugging the two boxes to his chest tightly.

Chapter Twelve

The hospital door opened a few inches, but Phoenix didn't notice it at first. She lay on her back, her head turned away, facing the wall. She was in the last stages of leukemia: her skin was parched and aged, with well-defined creases in her skin. She had nasal oxygen prongs, small tubes taped up her nose. Her hair was not made up; it was stringy, wet with sweat. Three I.V. bottles hung beside the bed, connected to a common tube to an artery on her arm. She had asked that the mirror be taken out of the room.

Phoenix turned her head and saw someone looking at her from the doorway. Her face screwed up in anguish. She tried to yell, but it came out a whisper.

"Oh, God, I *told* you not to do this!"

Slowly, guiltily, Griffin came on in the room, unsure about being there, then rushed forward and buried his face in her side, kneeling beside her bed.

She rolled her head from side to side on her pillow weakly, moving only as much as the tubes in her nose would allow. Her hand went to his hair and played with it for a few moments—that was the only movement in the stark white room.

"I told you not to do this . . ." she said softly. Griffin never raised his face from her side, but his hands groped for her and he held her.

"How did you find me?"

Griffin finally tried speech, but it came out as

quietly as when she spoke. "I called seventeen hospitals before . . ."

"Oh, God, Griffin, this is exactly what I didn't want to happen!" She rolled her head from side to side unhappily. "Go, Griffin, please, leave . . ." She tried to push him away, but she was too weak. He finally raised his head, and they looked at each other. She quickly turned away.

"What are you going to do?" Her voice got louder and started to crack. "You gonna buy me flowers? Make small talk? You want me to *save you a seat?*"

That was all she got out before the tears came.

"I just wanted to see you . . ."

"Please, Griffin, *please*. Just go."

Their hands and arms had intertwined, but Phoenix began shoving him away weakly with her hand.

But she realized the other hand held him tightly.

She pulled away from him completely, and he slowly stood up.

"Go . . . *please* . . ."

He took a step, but could go no further. He suddenly bent, gently turned her face toward him, bent over, and kissed her on the lips. He started to rise, but as he began to leave, she pulled him back, kissed him hard, then turned her head and shoved him away.

"Get out of her, Griffin." She softly cried into her pillow. "And don't ever come back."

Completely dazed, without looking back at her, Griffin slowly left the room.

Phoenix's hand curled up in a tight fist, twisting part of the bedsheet in a ball. The fierce grip continued on into the night, past lights out, until much later in the silent darkness when the fingers automatically uncurled from around the bedsheet.

FEBRUARY, 1976–LOS ANGELES

Griffin, in a suit and tie, leaned against his car fender, hands in his pockets, the wind blowing in his hair a little. It was a bright, sunny day, and he stared across the street at something, staring hard and not moving. Finally, almost ignoring the traffic around him, he walked across the street, down the sidewalk, and past a beautiful fountain beside the entrance to the cemetery.

A man gave him directions and Griffin wandered around, expressionless, emotionless, toward the general area through shady trees, green grass, and gray headstones.

He almost walked past it, then half-turned, stopped, and could only stare.

He saw a neat little tombstone which, in the usual deeply-engraved stone words, spelled out:

SARAH PHOENIX
1942–1976
P.S. Hi, Griffin. Thought
you'd probably drop by.

Reading the tombstone, Griffin's face reacted with several different emotions at once. He smiled in amusement—but his eyes became wet, threatening to overflow. He shook his head in disbelief, turned away, and then looked back again.

It was evening when he left, slowly walking back out through the cemetery, rubbing his eyes a little. The groundskeeper had turned on the sprinklers, and the sun was low in the sky, causing beautiful shadows and patterns on the green grass.

Griffin was just getting in his car when he noticed something on the front right side. It was the same tire as before, extremely flat.

Detached, without expression, Griffin went to the trunk, opened it, and routinely took out the jack and tire iron and walked back to the tire. He dropped the tire iron, which clanged noisily on the street, then happened to glance up at his windshield.

He saw his own helpless reflection looking back at him.

He sighed, looked away, looked around, then slowly raised the heavy tire iron and in one smooth, powerful move, smashed it down into his own windshield, splintering the face there into a thousand pieces of glass which flew out as the windshield cracked.

He smashed it again.

And again.

Until there was no glass left.

He turned and saw a small car parked in front of his.

In the back window, he saw the reflection of a man holding a tire iron.

He smashed it in, then moved around to the side of the car.

Still holding the tire iron in both hands, Griffin methodically, with an eerie blend of calmness and power, smashed both windows, then the windshield.

He looked up, saw about another ten cars parked down the street, and went on to the next. With the same powerful stroke, he brought the heavy tire iron down.

Glass exploded down into the car, up into the air, everywhere.

There were no pedestrians and little traffic, not that Griffin would have cared, anyway, since he kept moving from one car to the next, still methodically using the same powerful stroke, breaking in every piece of glass in every car on the street.

His face grew red, he began to sweat, and his hands and left cheek were cut from flying shards of glass, bleeding a little, but he routinely moved on to the next car, took his stance, and continued the same steady rhythm.

When he finished, he calmly walked back to his own car, wrapped his bleeding hand in his handkerchief, and fixed his flat tire. Griffin knew it was time to go home and try to tell his two sons about the importance of love and freight trains.

MARCH, 1976–LOS ANGELES

George Griffin sat in his brother's overstuffed chair, still holding the kite, still listening to the ocean waves outside the apartment. He took a final swallow from the can of beer, crushed it with one hand with uncharacteristic strength, and tossed it at the basketball goal over the wastebasket. He made it.

George stared at the small redwood box he had carried with him. He had set it down on the sofa, near the cardboard boxes of Griffin's cluttered mess. George went over to the box, opened it, and took out a small brass urn and stared at it.

He chuckled to himself.

"It *is* tacky . . ."

Laughing, cradling the heavy urn to his chest, George strode out of the apartment with long strides, as though he knew just where he was going.

The light plane was easy to rent, and the pilot was even easier to bribe, and before long, George was nudging the pilot and pointing down to a huge greenhouse below.

They made one low sweep over the big greenhouse, dipping low enough for George to see that there weren't any people at one end. It was all plants and glass benches, with the setting sun reflecting off the glass roof.

The plane made its turn, climbed a little, then dive-bombed toward the greenhouse, not unlike a B-29. George opened the door of the little plane, held out the urn, kissed it, then dropped it.

It turned over and over as it fell through the sky.

Inside the greenhouse, there was a terrible crashing sound like the world just ended, as the urn crashed through the glass roof, then kept right on going through several glass shelves and no small amount of potted rhododendrons, scaring the hell out of several people at the other end, making an ungodly noise which, strangely, sounded a little like music.

The small plane veered away, gaining altitude, serenely heading for home. Unnoticed by George or the pilot, they flew over a large water tower.

On the narrow little catwalk at the top of the water tower, an overweight man with a cigar in his mouth, wearing a gray uniform, was using a long roller to apply some dull gray paint to the water tower. As he finished painting over the huge Day-Glo "CLASS OF '59," he noticed something around on the right side of the tower, where Griffin had once been painting.

The city maintenance man looked disgusted as he saw a huge comical drawing of a heart with a crooked arrow through it. Inside, it said:

"Goddam kids," mumbled the workman, quickly reaching for more gray paint. If he hurried, he could be home in time to see part of the Rams game.

THE BEST OF BESTSELLERS
FROM WARNER BOOKS!

THE BERMUDA TRIANGLE MYSTERY—SOLVED
by Lawrence David Kusche   **(89-014, $1.95)**
Mr. Kusche has tracked down every last scrap of information on the infamous zone where numerous ships and planes have vanished. This book demonstrates that all those disappearances on which reliable information exists can be logically explained—or didn't occur in the Bermuda Triangle at all!

STRICTLY SPEAKING by Edwin Newman   **(79-898, $1.95)**
NBC-TV's Edwin Newman focuses on the sorry state of the English language as a reflection of the sorry state of society. "Relentlessly funny . . ."—**Chicago Tribune** AMERICA'S #1 BESTSELLER!

DEAD SOLID PERFECT by Dan Jenkins   **(79-817, $1.95)**
By the author of SEMI-TOUGH! Its hero is a swinging Texas golf pro whose off-links action is as hot and competitive as his play on the course. "Vintage Jenkins . . ."—**Newsweek**

THE WAR BETWEEN THE TATES   **(79-813, $1.95)**
by Alison Lurie
Fourteen weeks on **The New York Times** bestseller list! The brilliant, witty novel of a marriage under siege by young sex, middle age and old dreams. "A thing to marvel at . . . all that the novel was meant to be."—**The New York Times**

 A Warner Communications Company

Please send me the books I have checked.

Enclose check or money order only, no cash please. Plus 25¢ per copy to cover postage and handling N.Y. State residents add applicable sales tax.

Please allow 2 weeks for delivery.

WARNER BOOKS
P.O. Box 690
New York, N.Y. 10019

Name ....

Address ....

City .... State .... Zip ....

_____ Please send me your free mail order catalog